Always My Love

Dorothy Fletcher

CRIMSON
ROMANCE
F+W Media, Inc.

This edition published by
Crimson Romance
an imprint of F+W Media, Inc.
10151 Carver Road, Suite 200
Blue Ash, Ohio 45242
www.crimsonromance.com

ISBN 10: 1-4405-7190-2
ISBN 13: 978-1-4405-7190-9
eISBN 10: 1-4405-7189-9
eISBN 13: 978-1-4405-7189-3

One

Mike, the doorman at the big apartment house on Park Avenue in the East Seventies, watched the approach of the tall, slender, long-limbed girl who was crossing the avenue at the corner and heading for the building in front of which he stood taking advantage of the summer sun between duties.

The girl was Iris Easton, the young niece of one of the building's tenants, Mrs. Henry Collinge. Mrs. Collinge, whom Mike admired and respected, was every inch a lady, and the same was true of her niece. Iris Easton had the most beautiful manners, quite different from some of the sassy young girls you saw nowadays. Like her aunt, she was friendly, unassuming and sweet, really sweet.

She caught sight of him, waved and, as she came up to him, said as usual, "Hi, Mike, how's it going?"

He said it was going fine, thank you, but he knew she meant not only himself, but her aunt as well. Mrs. Henry Collinge had been a widow since the middle of last year, and her family—sister, brother-in-law and niece Iris—had rallied round, like the good people they were, never letting a week go by without one or all of them dropping in, or having her to dinner at their own house, which was not very far away.

Young Iris, in particular, played an important part in her aunt's life, was the most frequent visitor and generally spent several hours on a weekend day with Mrs. Collinge.

Mike had known her since she was a wee thing, had seen her grow from a child into a young girl and now a lovely young woman. She must be a great comfort to the childless—and now husbandless—woman upstairs, he often thought, and once again reflected on the girl's sweetness and kindness. So many girls lacked these fine qualities…they were too busy with their own selfish interests.

"See you later," Iris Easton said, and went inside to the lobby.

Turning, Mike saw her lithe form walking toward the elevators. A thoroughbred, he mused, and as adorable as any dewy Irish lass.

An Irish lad he was himself, though no longer in his prime, alas, and he was one of the very few Irish doormen left in New York. Once they had all been Gaelic, come to find a better life in the land of opportunity. Some of their children had made fortunes that were not to be sneezed at, or gone into politics and made a name for themselves.

Now, however, there were few of them left in attendance at these large and plush buildings. These days the accents were more likely to be Puerto Rican.

Mike, who had seen this particular house converted from rental to cooperative, knew pretty well what the purchase prices had been, and knew too that the Henry C. Collinge's had cost a good bit over $150,000…and that had been in pre-inflationary days.

He wondered—and knew Mrs. Collinge's niece wondered too—when Mrs. Collinge would get around to selling the place she was now rattling around in all alone. Alone, that was, except for Edith, her housekeeper.

Much too big for a widow lady. And no children of her own, poor soul. Of course Mr. C. had been so much older than Mrs. C. Such a young woman to be left alone!

He thought sagely, won't be all that long before she'll be snapped up by someone else. All that money Mrs. Collinge had been left…a rich widow would have plenty of chances.

Then again, maybe not. Everyone in the building had always talked about how loving the Collinges were toward each other. Holding hands on the street, like a couple of kids, and when the husband started failing…

He shook his head, vividly recalling the look of pain on Mrs. Collinge's face as her husband's steps faltered, and his face grew ashen, his body gaunt. Kept her head held high, though, kept the bright smile on her pretty face, with hardly a line or wrinkle in it.

A lovely lady, Mrs. Collinge. And rattling around in that great place upstairs…

• • •

Iris Easton hesitated, as she found herself doing these past long months, a finger indecisively poised over the bell on the door of 11C. For years there had been no hesitation. A firm press of the doorbell, then three sharp raps on the door itself…her own personal signal.

But that was before.

Before Uncle Henry died. And everything was different now. The happy days were over for Aunt Louisa, and though the greeting would be the same, the smile of welcome as bright, there was a falseness about it, a brittle determination, and a terrible emptiness.

You would have to know Aunt Louisa very well to detect the difference, though. Only those close to her—friends and family perceived the subtle change, the profound aura of sadness. On the surface, Louisa Collinge seemed the same brisk, positive personality she always had been, quick to make up her mind and quick to act. Outgoing, influential and exceedingly good-looking, her life had been cushioned by money…lots of it.

Louisa Collinge, in short, was very much the grande dame.

On those occasions when Iris dined out with her, in the very *best* eating places, Aunt Louisa invariably got the red carpet treatment and the most attentive service. It was like going to dinner with a duchess. Uncle Henry had called her "Princess."

Resolutely, Iris rang the bell, rapped the three times, and waited.

Edith let her in. Her aunt's housekeeper had skin the color of mahogany, a soft voice and a mind of her own. She was strong, capable, a magnificent cook and was, quite simply, a member of the family.

"Hello, darlin', come right on in. She's in the living room. How are you?"

"Hello, Edith. I'm fine. You?"

"Pretty good. So's she."

"That's nice."

Edith gave her an odd little look. "I mean she really is pretty good. You'll see. More like herself today."

"More like herself *how*?"

"Like she used to be. Before."

"*Really?*"

"Go and see for yourself. I've got something in the oven."

Edith went kitchenward and Iris passed through the room-sized foyer, into the living room beyond. This was one of the old-time apartment buildings, high-ceilinged and many-windowed, and of generous proportions.

There were lovely old pieces in this room, as there were in the others, for Louisa was a collector of antiques, so that over the years she had picked up many fine things.

Louisa herself, however, was not in the living room, so Iris wandered through to the bedroom in search of her. This was down a side hall, one of the many corridors in this spacious apartment.

"I'm here, where are you?" she called.

"Iris? Come in, I'm just finishing my toilette," her aunt's voice said in return, and there she was, in the dressing room with the chaise lounge and the luxurious, feminine appointments, sitting at her makeup table.

She was applying eye liner and, giving a quick smile to Iris's reflection in the mirror, completed the job with a few deft movements of her slim fingers.

Ever since she could remember, her aunt Louisa had been a role model for Iris. Louisa was a very pretty woman, not tall but well-proportioned. She had slightly uptilted eyes, which could be green or hazel, depending on what color she wore. Her face, like Iris's, was broad in the cheekbones and, like Iris's, tapered delicately at the chin.

She wore stunning, expensive clothes and had excellent legs, with small, fine-boned feet for which she had about a hundred pairs of shoes from places like Delman and Ferragamo. She had led a life of privileged ease, and it showed.

"There," Louisa said. "That's done and I'm presentable at last. I got up early enough, but then shilly shallied about doing odds and ends, and now look at the time. It's eleven-thirty, and Edith will have my head if lunch is delayed."

She turned, swung round and got up. "Hello, my darling," she said, and gave her niece a hug. "How's everything?"

"Fine. *You're* looking very well."

She does look better, Iris reflected. And she sounded better. That slight lilt to her voice…

"Let's go inside," Louisa said, and led the way to the living room. I want to have a little talk with you."

She sniffed. "Smells like a souffle, doesn't it? That means an early lunch, I daresay. Souffles do have a way of falling flat, so, dear, sit down and I'll get a few things off my chest."

Slightly mystified, but greatly heartened by what seemed a return of her aunt's old decisive manner, Iris sat, waiting. Louisa perched on the arm of a sofa, swinging one sleek leg.

She's so young-looking, Iris marveled, and then reminded herself that her aunt was, after all, only forty-six.

"Cigarette?" Louisa asked, holding out a silver box.

Iris shook her head, but her aunt lit one.

"Well then," she said. "I'll start by saying that for the past three days I've done nothing but cry. I scarcely went out at all.

I just moped about in this big place and wept. I had Edith in tears as well, poor thing. A long-delayed reaction, and something I'd wanted desperately to be able to do…but until now, couldn't manage. I, in effect, have cried myself out. And in doing so, am beginning to *feel* again. I was simply stony and bitter and angry, and I was enraged that I was still here, well and alive, while Henry was…was gone.

"I was…well, paralyzed, doing everything by rote, just going through the motions. Bitter I still am, I confess. But I've stopped being a zombie. I'm going to move. I'm determined about that. I'm going to *move*."

Iris looked about This apartment was a second home to her. Aunt Louisa was her mother's sister, and Iris had spent many a night and many weekends in this place.

Yet she and her parents had discussed it often. It was too big for Louisa, now she was alone. And the memories it must have for her aunt…

"Have you decided where you'll go?" I asked.

"France, since it's the country I know best."

It was more than a shock. It was like a physical blow. *France!* Of course Louisa had any number of friends there…but her only relatives were her sister, brother-in-law and niece, and they were *here*, in Manhattan.

"You mean you won't have an apartment here at all?" Iris asked blankly.

For a moment her aunt looked puzzled. Then, "Oh, Iris, I didn't mean move that way," she cried. "I just meant move, move *about*, stop pretending that everything is the same, being a robot, thinking, brooding, bemoaning my fate. When these things happen to us, we always react so characteristically. *Why me?* Well, it's always me, or he, or she. Tragedy strikes us all, sooner or later. And until you come to terms with that you're sunk. I've come to terms with it, Iris, at long last. It's been over a year since Henry died."

She gave a quick glance about the living room, with its treasures, some modest, some of very great value, and then looked back at Iris. "This is my home," she said. "I don't want to leave it. I don't want to lose its precious ghosts, the priceless recollections of the happy days we've had in this place. Oh no, I'll stay here."

Then she laughed, an almost excited little laugh. "I meant, darling, that I'll travel again. Oh, I know I've said to myself a hundred times that I couldn't bear to go without…"

As if testing herself, she said the words she probably hadn't voiced aloud before. "Without Henry," she finished. "Our trips abroad together were like a never-never land, two adventurous spirits setting forth. But I won't wither and rot. I'm too proud for that. I've mollycoddled myself quite enough. Now it's time to pick up the pieces and go on with the business of living."

"I'm glad," Iris said quietly. "And so proud of you. I couldn't love you more if you were my own mother."

That did bring a film of tears to her aunt's eyes and, with Iris's eyes moist as well, they looked at each other across the space of the enormous room and then, walking toward each other to meet in an embrace, they clung together.

I suddenly feel that I'm the older, and she's the child to comfort, Iris thought, and then Edith's voice, from the doorway, broke the emotional moment.

"Lunchtime," she announced. "So break it up, you two, and come get it while it's hot."

• • •

It was when they were having coffee in the living room later on that Louisa said, "What I want very much is for you to come with me to Europe, Iris."

"But—"

"Not to keep me company, I don't mean that. I'm not plumping for a substitute…someone to take Henry's place. And I know you have only a regulation vacation from your job. Two weeks, or is it three?"

"I can usually manage three. But—"

"Iris, as I said, I've had plenty of time for thought in the past year. Hear me out, won't you?"

"Okay."

"Darling, it's no secret that Henry was a very rich man, and that he's left me a very rich woman. Your job is a quite decent one, but…well, it's not precisely a career job, and…"

She bit her lip, reflecting. "The thing is that I don't really peg you as a career woman, any more than I was…am. And dear—"

Iris said it for her without rancor, though not with any particular enthusiasm. "I'm not getting any younger?" she suggested.

Her aunt smiled. "Well, that's one way of putting it, though not the way I would have done. Yes, the years do have a way of racing on, but I wasn't really thinking of the fact that you're a month away from being twenty-four and not involved in a meaningful relationship."

She was treading on dangerous ground and she knew it. The fact that her niece had dates aplenty and a ready escort for any social event that might present itself was because Iris was stunning-looking and a logical target for any eager male eye.

But Iris, a little over a year and a half ago, had had her own tragedy. She had been engaged to a man ten years older than herself, a fine-looking, substantial type, ambitious and serious. Mark Pawling gave every indication of being exactly what Iris thought he was…very nearly perfect. The girl's parents, as well as Louisa and Henry, considered him a "sterling" young man.

And then, with no warning at all, the engagement had been abruptly broken. Iris was thrown over in favor of a girl four years older than Mark, and not very attractive at that. Her father, the head of the company Mark worked for, had thereupon bestowed a vice-presidency on his future son-in-law.

It had been Iris's first lesson in pragmatism…and that it had left deep scars was no secret to Louisa.

She had suffered for her niece, observed the cynicism that had been the inevitable consequence and was just as unhappy about Iris's reactions as was her sister Virginia, Iris's mother. It was as if Iris had anesthetized herself, cut off all deeper feelings and sealed herself in a kind of protective cocoon.

She was popular, dated frequently but casually, and had her fun, but she seemed to have written romance off as a lost cause.

Louisa was bending the truth when she told Iris that she wasn't thinking of her niece's approaching her twenty-fourth birthday without being romantically involved. Because she *was* thinking of it. To her mind, there were only so many years to deal with. You were young, you were middle-aged, and you were old. It was as simple as that.

Louisa, being childless, was as concerned about Iris's future as if she had been her own daughter. To see her niece drifting, without any shining promise in view, hurt her immeasurably. If someone had asked Louisa what she considered a deadline for the proper marriageable age, she would have said, without any hesitation, "Why, twenty-five, of course."

Louisa, naturally, was of another generation. Things had changed a bit…but not for the better she had decided. The old truths were the real truths, she insisted. Men and women were meant to merge, build together…therein lay true happiness.

She regarded her niece with frank and unconcealed admiration. Iris Easton was, to her mind, the most beautiful girl she had ever encountered. Part of it might be, she conceded, pure prejudice. This was her sister's offspring and she adored her sister.

But she was sure that Iris was someone special. Louisa had friends with daughters, marvelous-looking young women with a Manhattan panache and private school manners. But Iris, with her abundance of honey-colored hair, soft brown eyes, straight little nose, short upper lip and full lower one, could have been painted by Sargent if their times had coincided.

Yet since the debacle of the broken engagement, Iris had become cautious, distrustful and *distressingly* independent. Louisa was beginning to despair.

"You were saying?" her niece prompted.

"I don't remember what I was saying," Louisa confessed.

"Something about my not being cut out for a career woman."

"Do you want a career?"

There was a trace of impatience. "How do I know?" Then, reflectively, "How does anyone know?"

"I imagine people like Gloria Steinem knew. Or Betty Friedan. Or some woman politician, like Shirley Chisholm."

"Maybe."

"Anyway, somehow I've gone off the track. Let's get back to my having quite a bit of money and wanting to take you abroad. Everything I have, Iris, will go to you. No, don't shake your head in that *irritating* way! To whom else would I leave it? To you and Edith, of course. So why shouldn't you share in it now, instead of everything later? Have some present joy of it. What I'd really like is—"

She considered and then went ahead. "What I'd really like is for you to quit your job and travel with me indefinitely. This year, next year, and..."

She saw that the answer would be a regretful no. Smoothly, she continued. "If not that, then for your vacation this year. You said you could manage three weeks. We'll go anywhere you like. I mentioned France, but it could be anywhere. Italy, Spain... whatever. You've never been to Europe, though Henry and I so much wanted to take you. It didn't happen because I just didn't think it would be fair to…"

She felt a little self-conscious. "Well, to offer you something your own parents would have liked to but just couldn't afford. Your mother is so *damned* difficult to do things for!"

"She's proud…like you," Iris pointed out. "I know they had some hard times, but they put me through Barnard and are pleased as punch that they did it without any help. Oh, I waitressed, and took other odd jobs, but that was only a drop in the bucket."

She gave her aunt a fond look. "If I were someone different," she said, "I'd fall in line with your first suggestion. Quit my job and be…say, your companion. Only, I can't. You knew that right away, I saw it in your face. We're very close, you and I, and it's a great joy to me. I've told you things I've never even told my parents. We have a very special kind of relationship. I love the Cinderella story you outlined for me…the idea of my giving up a not very interesting job and being…"

She grinned. "Beautiful People, traveling the world with a glamorous aunt. If I were five years older, I might take you up on it. Right now, though…"

She lit an unaccustomed cigarette and went on. "But as for three weeks in Europe, why not? I have a little over fifteen hundred in my savings account, and that ought to cover expenses. When did you plan to leave?"

Her aunt's face tightened. "I thought I had made it clear," she said shortly. "Either I take you and pay for your trip or it's no go. I'm sorry, Iris, but that's a condition."

"But I have the money!"

"Forgive me for being just a little bit angry, but on no account will I stand for it. I will not impoverish you. Either I have you as my guest or the deal's off."

She raised her hand peremptorily before her niece had a chance to answer. "I have nothing," she said quietly. "Nothing at all now, except for a lot of money. If I can't use some of it for someone else's benefit, then it's a hateful thing."

She sat back. "It's up to you, love."

"That's it?"

"That's it."

"I'll think about it."

"No," Louisa said vehemently. "I'm about to make my plans. I have to know now. Yes or no. As I said, it's up to you."

Iris got up and went to the window. It was true her aunt was a very rich woman. Whatever cost Iris would be to her on this little junket would be peanuts, considering the size of Louisa's inheritance. Why was it that she felt obligated, why did she hesitate? She loved this woman, who was like a second mother to her.

I guess I'm proud too, she thought.

She looked back at her aunt.

Louisa, who only a short while back was so bereft, so frozen with grief, was once again the old Louisa, the unwavering, decisive person Iris had known from babyhood. She seemed to have come into her own again, was once more the calm, decision-making individual that was the real, familiar Aunt Louisa.

Was she to hamper her aunt's recovery by refusing to allow her this small indulgence?

"The answer is yes," she said finally.

"On my conditions?"

Iris nodded.

"Talk about pulling teeth," Louisa said, her face breaking into a broad smile. "Well, that's more like it. Come give me a kiss."

"And thank you," Iris said, as they each sat down again. "It's a lovely treat you're offering me."

"*My* treat, *my* pleasure," her aunt corrected, glowing. "Now I thought we'd leave around the beginning of September. Europe is at its best then, after most of the tiresome tourists have gone home. Iris, where shall we go?"

"You said France."

"Would you rather it be somewhere else?"

"France suits me fine," Iris said fervently. "There are many places I would like to go before I die, but of them all, France heads the list."

"Then we'll fly to Paris, and after that play it by ear." She hugged herself. "What a joy it will be to have you with me!"

"And I'm glad you're…better."

"I have to be better. Life, as they say, must go on. It's just that I've at last been able to reconcile to that."

She got up briskly. "I've some travel folders for you saved from previous trips. You must take them home and browse over them. You should be traveling with someone your own age, of course, but we'll have our own fun. I can't wait to show you…oh, everything."

She went to the beautiful old escritoire that was a piece from the eighteenth century, opened it, and drew out a thick sheaf of brochures. Putting them into a large manila envelope she handed them to Iris. "There's a marvelous walking map of Paris here," she said. "If you really study it carefully, you'll find that when you get there you'll know where the main points of interest are."

"I'll certainly do that."

"And, Iris, I know so many people there who would have sons about your age. You'll be able to go dancing, or to the films, and—"

Iris's face changed quickly, became wary. She looked away and then swiftly back. "Auntie, you're not going to try to matchmake, are you?"

She really seemed distressed, Louisa thought, and her own reactions were both compassionate and exasperated. Really, this girl did try her patience sometimes. What normal young woman could object to being introduced to men who were the sons of family friends, for heaven's sake? What girl wouldn't jump at the chance to be taken to Parisian discos and boites?

Was her niece *ever* going to rise above that sordid business with Mark Pawling, and begin the business of living again? Just be a happy, eager young girl…

She was a little short with Iris. "No," she said. "I've no intention of doing anything like that. A little Paris night life wouldn't hurt you, but it's up to you. Don't worry, I won't twist your arm, Iris."

Contrition showed in her niece's face. "Forgive me, but it's just that I must go at my own pace. For the moment, I'm content to drift with the tide. *Laissez faire,* you understand. Anyway, it's you I want to be with."

"Whatever you say. I just want you to enjoy your trip."

"You are an understanding dear," Iris said gratefully.

And when she left her aunt's apartment, she was in a blissful daze. Europe this early fall…France…Paris…

"And how is your dear aunt today?" Mike asked her on her way out.

"Oh, so much better."

"I was a bit worried about her," he confided, "seeing as how I haven't laid eyes on her in several days."

"She's…passed the crisis, as they say, Mike. Much improved. And thanks for worrying about her."

"I like her you know. She's a lady, a real lady."

Yes, she was, Iris thought, as she walked on home. Her Aunt Louisa was truly to the manor born.

Two

If Virginia Easton had ever envied her sister Louisa her good luck in snagging a husband who had made an early fortune in plastics, it had been only in periods of stress in her own household. There *had* been such periods, and at times she had despaired of providing the kind of college education she considered Iris's due. Tears had been shed and hands had been wrung, but things had "come out all right," and although Virginia had a host of friends and acquaintances, the person who meant the most to her (aside from her husband and daughter) was her sister Louisa.

What had prevented her from ever taking a penny from Louisa, or even borrowing, was the fact that the balance, she felt, must be kept even. Louisa had the money—and a great deal of it—while she, Virginia, had the child, the daughter fate had denied her sister. Louisa, after a second miscarriage, was unable to have children and it had been a great sorrow to her. One reason, perhaps, why she had so cherished and loved what she did have…her husband, who was twenty years older than herself.

And now, with Henry dead, the balance was uneven. In spite of her wealth, Louisa had, substantially, nothing while Virginia had everything…husband, daughter and for the first time in her life, some financial comfort. Virginia's own world seemed suddenly blighted. With Louisa's life shattered, her own was in chaos as well.

So when Iris came home that Saturday afternoon to announce that Aunt Louisa was immeasurably improved, and "picking up the pieces," it was like a kind of rebirth. Suddenly the sun had its full strength again, the faces of her loved ones, husband George and daughter Iris, swam into her consciousness to dazzle and enchant her, and the new living room sofa that had seemed much too costly when it had been bought filled her with a joy and pleasure that set her to straightening its cushions about a dozen times.

"Beautiful thing," she murmured to it. "You are worth every penny and I love you dearly."

"And we're to leave in September," Iris told her.

"Isn't that wonderful!"

Dad said, as they were having their supper, "I'm not disapproving, Iris. You're in a way, like a child of her own. Perfectly proper for her to underwrite your vacation…at this particular sad time, anyway."

"Iris wouldn't do anything you'd disapprove of, George, so no need to take that *ensouffrance* tone."

"Am I being taken down a peg or two?" he asked mildly.

His wife beamed at him. "Say anything you have a mind to. I feel very happy tonight."

"I'm enormously fond of Louisa Collinge myself, and if I hadn't been guarded carefully from a glimpse of her while we were courting, I might very well have married her myself."

"She wouldn't have had you."

"Why?" he asked reasonably.

"Because it would have been over my dead body, and then you'd have gone to prison."

"I was that fascinating?"

"Very likely just to me, and I would have slain to keep you."

"In that case you'd have gone to prison," Iris pointed out.

"And gladly so."

"You're really quite a pair," Iris commented.

Her mother caught the wistfulness in her daughter's voice, and thought, damn Mark Pawling for what he did to my child.

"So you'll be going abroad, Iris," George Easton said, and looked across at his wife. "You and I will have our turn one of these days," he told her. "We had a rather hard row to hoe, but things are looking up."

He reached for her hand and squeezed it. "You've been a good and patient wife, and I love you very much."

Iris, touched, thought that to have a man say something like that to you would be better than all the riches in the world, better than anything life could ever offer.

They left for Paris on the first week in September. Iris's current beau drove them all out to the airport. His name was Jeffrey Hamm and Mother—who was as eager to see her daughter go to the altar and "settle down" as was Aunt Louisa—had said once, "If you and Jeff married, Iris, you'll never be able to name your first-born after me, should it be a girl."

"Why not?"

"Would you name a child Virginia Hamm?"

But she knew her daughter was no more serious about Jeff than she was about any of the men she dated nowadays.

Jeffrey was disturbed because Iris was to be away for such a chunk of time. "How about hurrying back?" he suggested, looking quite dejected.

"I haven't even gone yet," Iris said.

She liked him. He was decent, intelligent and quite a bit of fun. There had been others she had liked. But only one who had lit the flame in her.

Mark Pawling…

Was there to be only one in a lifetime?

"It won't be all that long," she said. "And I *will* miss you, Jeff."

"Take care of yourself," he said huskily.

Then their flight was called. Final good-byes were hastily exchanged, Mother saying, "You've got the Lomotil? Be sure to take it if there's the slightest sign of an upset stomach."

It was eight o'clock of a bright, still summery evening, with the sky still showing traces of a faint pink. Iris, boarding the plane, looked quickly back and, as she did, a burst of rosy brilliance flushed the heavens and then, just as swiftly, died down.

Like a salute, she thought, and then walked through the doors.

•••

They arrived at Charles de Gaulle Airport at seven in the morning.

First there was, upon awakening from a restful slumber which, in first class, was a little easier to come by than in second, an orange dawn. A strange, eerie glory that was unlike anything Iris had ever seen before. She gazed at it, fascinated and bemused, until the bizarre color faded and gave way to a pearly, early morning.

Her aunt was still asleep, her legs tucked up in her chair. Iris rose quietly and made her way to the washroom. She had taken her cosmetic case and was able to brush her teeth, wash her face and comb out her tousled hair.

When she went back down the aisle, some of the passengers were beginning to come alive, rousing themselves from their night's doze, shifting stiffly in their seats. One woman groaned audibly, muttered something to her companion, a man, and struggled up. She walked down the aisle and disappeared into a washroom.

With a slight sigh, Louisa opened her eyes.

"Good morning," Iris said.

"Good morning, dear. Did you sleep?"

"Yes, quite decently."

"So did I. My word, you look refreshed. You've been to the washroom, haven't you? Perfectly groomed and combed. And I, all sags and wrinkled panty hose."

She got up. "I'll go make some repairs of my own. I smell breakfast preparations, so I'd better be quick about it."

While she was gone, Iris busied herself with her money converter. One franc was equal roughly to twenty cents. Therefore five francs was equal to a dollar, depending, of course, on the condition of the American dollar. She was starting out with a Quick Pack of forty dollars, which should give her a small start. For additional, there were two hundred dollars in traveler's checks.

"Counting your wealth?" Louisa asked, returning to her seat.

"Like a miser. Look at all that loot."

Her aunt laughed. "That wouldn't get you very far."

Breakfast came shortly after that, and shortly after *that* the loudspeaker crackled.

"This is your captain speaking. Landing will be in one half hour. The sky is clear above Paris, the temperature is 78 degrees. We hope you have enjoyed your flight. Thank you."

Then it was repeated in French. *"Mesdames et Messieurs..."*

Fifteen minutes later the overhead lights flashed for seatbelts to be fastened and cigarettes doused.

Then the plane started its slow descent. In no time at all the plains and valleys of France swam into view below them—neat rows of wheat and grain on the farmlands, miniature trees, squares of varying colors—and then the Seine, like a silver ribbon winding its way across the broad expanse.

They touched down with a velvety little bump and whooshed across the runway.

"Well," Louisa said, "here we are."

The sun, blazing in through the windows, was dazzling.

"Thank God for small favors," Louisa said, unzipping her seat belt. "It's a lovely, warm day. One's first glimpse of Paris should always be on a lovely, warm day."

She got up, smoothed her skirt, and stretched luxuriously. "We're getting off to a good start," she said and, with Iris following, made her way to the exit door.

Three

That they were not staying at the Ritz was a welcome surprise to Iris. The Ritz, of course, would be gorged with American and English personalities of ancient vintage and horrid, rich Germans who would snap their fingers at waiters.

"Oh no," Louisa said when Iris commented on it. "We never put up at the Ritz. Not the Paris Ritz, at any rate. We used to stay at the Bristol, but decided it had too much *side,* and one day we found a tiny little hotel just around the corner from the Ritz and have made it our Paris home ever since."

She had pointed out notable landmarks on the ride from the airport, once they had passed through the dreary industrial districts that preceded their entry into Paris proper, and said suddenly, "Now we're on the Rue St. Honoré, which leads into the Place Vendôme."

The taxi driver made a right turn and they were at their destination, the Place Vendôme, of which Iris had seen many a picture postcard. No replica could do it justice, she thought; it was an almost austere, stately square of superb proportions, a sublime example of seventeenth century artistry in a city that offered many such architectural wonders.

At its center, a granite column on a monumental pedestal rose magisterially, topped by the statue of Napoleon Bonaparte.

"And here's our little hotel," Louisa said, as the cab's driver pulled up, with a screech of tires, to the curb.

They climbed out of the taxi and the driver began pulling their luggage from the trunk of the vehicle. Then a fresh-faced young boy in uniform came out and stood waiting for the baggage.

Louisa opened her handbag, drew out some French notes and asked the young *portier,* with a pretty smile, to please pay their driver.

"And now let's go inside and get ourselves settled," she said to Iris, and swept through the opened glass doors.

Her niece smiled affectionately. Her aunt was every inch the seasoned traveler.

It was indeed a small hotel, with a small and discreetly correct lobby, and at the desk the concierge, exclaiming with what appeared to be a very sincere pleasure when Louisa greeted him, came out from behind his desk, said he was enchanted to see her once again this year, and started ordering the young boy who by this time had lugged in their suitcases, to be quick about it.

"*Vite, vite,*" he cried, and dashed behind the desk again for the keys to their rooms.

"And be sure everything is in order," he told the uniformed *portier.* "Madame is a favored client."

"Pierre, this is my niece, Iris Easton," Louisa said.

"Hello, Pierre."

"*Enchanté,* Mademoiselle. Welcome to Paris."

"*Merci,* Pierre."

They surrendered their passports and followed the *portier* to the elevator, getting out at the fourth floor.

He opened a door halfway down the hall, stood aside, and they walked inside.

It was a suite, with a bedroom and bath for each, and in between a lovely little salon. The ceilings were high, as were the windows with their airy ninon curtains and handsome tapestry drapes. The furnishings were modified Louis Seize, and the room light and cheerful. There were good prints on the walls; the bull's-eye mirror with its eagle mounting, Recamier sofa in front of which was a long coffee table and baroque wall sconces all added up to a very homey living room.

Louisa was busy separating the bags. "These are mine," she told the young boy. "The others belong in my niece's room."

After a while everything was sorted out and Louisa bade Iris go and see if her room was shipshape. Her luggage deposited and at last alone, Iris stood in the middle of her room and looked about. The same tall, almost ceiling-high windows in here too, and the bathroom was larger than her room at home. Larger by far, and with a tub that could have accommodated someone six feet by seven.

She went back to the bedroom and sank down on the queen-sized bed, felt its incredible comfort, patted its two fat pillows, got up again and sat in each of the four small gilt chairs, went to the desk and pulled out the center drawer, where there was Hotel Vendôme stationery and then went to the windows.

The sun winked at her. She winked back. "Hello, Paris sun," she said to it, and then regarded the telephone that sat on a bedside table.

"I wish I could call someone," she said aloud.

Or better yet, she wished someone would call her. Right now, right this minute. Someone who would say, "Hello, pet, so you finally got here…Why not meet me at the Marignon for lunch? There's so much to talk about…"

No one would call her, of course. No one knew her here. People would call her aunt, but not her.

Maybe some day…

She went back to the salon.

"Is your room all right?" Louisa asked.

"It's fantastic," Iris said.

"That's good," her aunt said. "You'll probably want to freshen up before we start out."

"Start out?"

"Yes, of course. What else? I thought we'd have lunch at Yar's, a Russian place Henry and I always liked. First have a look around, you know."

"But don't you want a nap or something? I mean, after that long plane ride?"

"Darling, I'm not exactly in my dotage! Henry and I, after settling in a bit, always started right out *doing* things. I thought, since you're a stranger here, we'd walk up to the Rue de Rivoli, just a block and a half away, and look in some of the lovely shops there. Then head over to the Rue de l'Opéra and give you some Paris atmosphere." She smiled fondly. "Are you happy to be here, Iris?"

"Oh, Auntie, I can't tell you! I'm in seventh heaven."

"Then shower and change, and I'll give you an hour or so. Then come out again, all fresh and rosy, and we'll go adventuring. And bring your camera, since you'll certainly want to have snapshots of your first day here."

The day passed in a kind of blur. A glorious blur, to be sure, but for a newcomer like Iris, impressions were necessarily jumbled and kaleidoscoped.

The main impact was of an incredibly beautiful city, a city that actually seemed to glitter. Iris was overwhelmed with its shimmer, with the breathtaking uniformity of its mansard-roofed skyline, the many lacy bridges over the Seine, and the river itself, flowing its timeless way below the embankments. The vast sky, blooming with fast-moving clouds, seemed different from other skies. Its color was paler, more diffuse, varying from an almost washed-out blue to a deeper cobalt, and the whole effect subtly elusive.

How to describe it?

Why try? she thought. This was the sky the Impressionists had painted…Corot, Monet, Vuillard, Seurat…

Her first day was wonderful…and exhausting. Emotion played its part. Tears, at unbidden moments, rose astonishingly. This was Paris…city of her dreams.

At six they returned to the hotel, weary from jet lag and a long day's outing, and Louisa proposed a drink in the bar lounge on the second floor.

It was a pleasant room, with easy chairs and oak furniture. Not very large, but sizeable enough to accommodate about forty people. There was a mirrored bar at the rear and a man behind it who raised a hand in greeting as they walked toward a table.

He soon came over.

"*Bon soir,*" he said warmly. "I am so happy to see you once again. I missed you very much last year."

"You know that—" Louisa started to say, and the man interrupted with a quiet, "Yes, I know, of course. I am so sorry."

"Thank you, Marcel. I'd like to introduce my niece, Iris Easton, my sister's daughter."

"*Enchanté,* Mademoiselle," the man said. "Your first trip to Paris?"

"Yes."

"You arrived only today. Have you formed any impressions?"

"Yes, I think it's wonderful."

"I am glad. A martini for you, Madame?"

"Your memory never fails you. Yes, Marcel, and for my niece too. *Très sec,* as usual."

"I know," he said, with a smile. "A mere whisper of the vermouth."

They stayed for only half an hour in order to have some rest in their rooms before foraying out to dinner. Three tables had been occupied since they had come in, none with English-speaking persons. All were French except for two gentlemen who sounded Russian to Iris. She was almost sure she heard one of them say "*Nyet.*"

"I'm glad we're staying here," she told her aunt. "And I'm mad about the Place Vendôme. It's so historyish."

"It used to be horribly disfigured by automobiles cluttering it up," Louisa said. "It was, I assure you, one big parking lot. But then they built an enormous underground garage and now it's the way it should be."

She looked toward the bar and caught Marcel's attention. He brought over the bill for their drinks, and Louisa signed for it.

"Have an enjoyable evening," Marcel said cordially as they left. "And Mademoiselle, welcome to Paris. I wish you happiness here."

They were no sooner in their quarters than the telephone rang in Louisa's room.

"You go in and lie down for, say, half an hour," she told Iris. "We should leave here at around seven-thirty or so for dinner. Excuse me, I must answer that."

Iris, needing no coaxing, went right to her bedroom. She closed the door, stripped off her clothes and slipped into the comfort of the wide bed. She set her alarm for seven and fell instantly into a delicious slumber.

The next thing she knew there was a voice that seemed to come from very far away.

"Iris…"

Her eyes opened reluctantly. "What?" she mumbled.

"It's twenty past seven."

The voice was that of her Aunt Louisa, who was sitting on the edge of her bed and running a hand through her hair.

"Too tired for dinner?" Louisa asked.

"No. Gee. I'm sorry. I set the alarm, but I guess I didn't hear it go off." She leaned on an elbow. "Who was that on the phone?"

"A friend of mine. Sure you're up to getting dressed and going out for a meal?"

"Yes, of course. I won't be a minute."

"Half an hour will do. The restaurant we're going to is very near here."

"Okay."

She showered quickly and was dressed at a few minutes before eight. There was only a short walk to *Chez Tante Louise,* the place Louisa had in mind.

When they arrived, it was readily evident that it was a restaurant in which her aunt and uncle had dined frequently, judging from the cordial greetings that were extended.

Tante Louise, which was almost the name of Iris's aunt, might have been a pet haunt for obvious reasons, her niece decided. In any event, it was a delightful place, quietly comfortable and not overly formal.

The food was excellent and the wine, a light, buoyant Beaujolais, a perfect accompaniment.

"This is the kind of eating place Henry and I always liked," Louisa said. "You know Henry was always averse to splash and we never went in for flamboyant restaurants or anything else showy. We were always partial to these quiet, relaxing atmospheres and mostly avoided spots like *Lasserve,* or *Véfour.* Maybe it's an inverse snobbery, but it's how we always felt."

"It's okay with me," Iris said, "as I'm sure you must know. I'd just as soon eat in our rooms—a bottle of wine and some deli stuff."

"We'll probably resort to that too, if we should be too dragged out after a long and arduous day, to face dolling ourselves up and going out.

"And anyway," she added, "I must watch my weight. You don't have to worry, you gorgeous, skinny thing. But I do, and I must get on the scales tomorrow."

"You don't weigh any more than I do."

"Maybe not, but it's all in the wrong places."

They were back at the Place Vendôme at a little after ten. The splendid square, now gloriously floodlit, was deserted. It looked noble, and somber, and magnificent. The warmth of the day had become a clear and still, faintly chilly night.

It seemed a pity to go in, and leave all that beauty.

"I had a wonderful day," Iris said, when they were upstairs. "There will be other days, but this one, my very first, will never, ever be forgotten."

"I'm so glad. Give us a kiss, and then beddy-bye."

Aunt Louisa had said that when she was just a little kid. *Give us a kiss and then beddy-bye...*

Then both of them closed their doors and Iris, dead for sleep, cleaned her teeth and climbed into the sack.

Those two fat pillows, linen-sheathed, were like heaven itself, and the window, opened almost all the way, brought in Parisian night breezes, foreign zephyrs that smelled, faintly, of hyacinth.

Or so Iris imagined.

She slept dreamlessly. Or, if there were dreams, they failed to surface when she awoke to a bright Paris sky and turned over, eagerly, to greet the morning sun that rayed over her bed and bathed her in its brilliance.

She remembered her Baudelaire, and said aloud, *"De tirer de mon soleil de mon coeur, et de faire des mes pensers brûlants une tiède atmosphère..."*

So there, she thought triumphantly. Her French courses hadn't been a total loss. Then, throwing back the covers, she got up and took a cold, bracing shower.

Four

"I thought we'd go to Notre Dame today," Louisa said, over café au lait and croissants in the sunny salon.

"Great, just what I'd like most to do."

"Suppose we start at the Concorde, cross the river, walk up to the Quai des Grands Augustins, have a look in some of the antique shops there, and reach the cathedral by crossing back at the Pont St. Michel. There are many ways to get there on foot, but that way is one of my favorite walks."

"Sounds lovely."

It was. The sun blazed, though it was a bit on the coolish side, calling for sweaters. It was a long, leisurely trek, and riverside, with the Seine sparkling and clear. Boats glided on its surface, with the occasional white triangle of a sail limned enticingly.

When they came to the Quai des Grands Augustins, there were any number of shops that vended antiques, their gleaming plate-glass windows awninged against the sun. Louisa didn't buy anything, though she looked into several of them, and in one saw a Boulle clock she told the owner she would "think about."

Then they went on, and Louisa said that shortly they would come to the bookstalls. "If you're lucky, Iris, you might find a rare first edition in all the welter. Though you'd have to be very lucky indeed."

The bookstalls on the banks of the Seine…that, Iris thought eagerly, was something she had very much looked forward to. Someone had said that the bookseller on the quays represented one of the most authentic figures of everyday life in Paris. And very soon, there they were, lined up on the embankment, their lathed green over-covers shading books, prints and posters.

Iris lost herself completely, searching avidly for some bibliophilic find which would be like looking for a needle in a haystack. There were hundreds and hundreds of tomes, some deliciously musty with age, others modern fiction not worth glancing at.

It would take time and patience to sift through this mass of reading material. Yet it would be exciting to come across a real treasure.

"Find anything of interest?" her aunt finally asked.

Her niece looked slightly dazed. "Give me several months and maybe I can unearth something that will make my heart beat faster."

"Or several years," Louisa said sympathetically. She looked at her watch. "Give it up for now. I thought we'd have a coffee at that cafe over there."

"All right, it would be nice to sit down for a bit."

They walked across to an inviting plaza that was marked by one of the ubiquitous cobalt-blue signs. Place St. Michel, the sign said, and the cafe's outdoor adjunct presented an attractive view of the surrounding area.

They chose a table on the outer circumference, where they could sit in the sun, rather than under the canopy. Iris shrugged out of her sweater.

Louisa looked at her watch again. Iris smiled. "Do you really care about time?" she asked. "I don't. I've forgotten the meaning of it."

"Time is relative," Louisa replied. "It can be important or not, depending on circumstances."

"That sounds profound."

"Does it? How nice. Where are you going?"

"To find a john. Will you excuse me?"

"Can't you wait until we order?"

"I won't be long. *Café noir* for me, if the waiter comes over."

She got up and weaved her way among tables and then went inside. It was a busy place and rather noisy, with a television going full blast over the bar. Looking about, Iris saw no helpful signs, so she asked a passing waiter.

"Ou est la lavabo, s'il vous plait?"

"Par là," he said, and pointed.

She found it, used it, and came out again.

It was only a little after eleven o'clock in the morning, but the place was lively. Waiters flitted about, their trays held high. Tables were occupied by beer-drinking and wine-tippling customers. There was also the smell of cooking, with the odor of onions prevalent. Even at this early hour, a few people had quantities of food on their plates, some of them mopping up a dark, thick gravy with bits of bread. Silverware clattered and glasses tinkled.

Iris skirted some people just entering, nearly collided with a harried looking waiter, and gained the doorway.

She was making her way between the outdoor tables again when a thought struck her. This was the Place St. Michel…so then the Boulevard St. Michel must begin at this point. Why, of course!

The famed "Boul' Mich'," which led to the Sorbonne and the student quarter.

The Sorbonne…where she had so wanted to spend one of her college years.

There was suddenly a hand on her arm.

"You have lost something," a voice said and, turning, Iris found herself face to face with a dark-eyed man who was holding out a highly-colored pamphlet.

She recognized it as one of her own, and for a moment stared stupidly at it. Her handbag—a large, roomy tote—was hooked over her shoulder. There was an open pocket on one side, stuffed with her tourist paraphernalia.

She looked up quickly. That brochure couldn't possibly have fallen out of her tote. The pocket was deep. There was no way she could have lost it.

Yes, one way…and the only way. This man had deliberately "lifted" it from the pocket in the bag in order to speak to her.

She gave him a rapid, comprehensive glance.

He was French: his accent testified to that. Besides, he *looked* French—slightly aquiline nose, very dark eyes that were nearly black, and the same dark, inky hair. Handsome…in a European way, and with a smile that was faintly amused.

Or insolent, she thought.

He was tall, taller than she by a good bit, whereas height was generally not an attribute of the French. He was dressed casually, in a striped shirt that was open at the neck, cocoa-colored pants that were snug and a bit faded, and there was a very large watch on his left wrist.

She judged him to be in his early thirties.

"Thanks," she said, and took the brochure from his outstretched hand. *"Merci beaucoup."*

"Rien. You speak French very well."

She had to smile at that. She had spoken only two words of French. He was making quite a try, this young boulevardier.

She didn't answer, simply nodded, and headed once more for the table where her aunt was sitting and watching the little confrontation.

She didn't get very far. A hand was again on her arm.

"You could have told me that I speak English well," he said with mock reproach.

"You speak English well," she answered obligingly, and looked pointedly down at the hand on her arm, a tanned hand with a soft stroking of dark hair at the wrist.

"I like very much to keep in practice," he told her. "To converse with Americans."

"Americans speak a different kind of English," she said. "Better practice with English girls."

"American is just as important as English," he assured her.

This time she shook herself free. "Thanks again," she said firmly, and walked away.

She reached their outside table and grinned at her aunt as she sat down. "My first pickup," she murmured. "He tried his best, I will say that for him."

She waited for her aunt's giggle. Instead, there was a frown on Louisa's face, and a kind of displeased expression.

"Oh, don't worry, things like that don't bother me, Auntie. Imagine it, he must have pulled this right out of my bag. Said I'd lost it."

She stuffed the brochure back where it belonged. She resisted an impulse to look back and see if the man was still around, and then was annoyed at herself for giving him a second thought.

"You didn't have to be so distant," her aunt said quietly.

"Distant?" She was honestly surprised.

"Unfriendly. Remember, we're foreigners here. When someone whose country this is makes a cordial overture the least you can do is meet him half way."

"Half *way?* Why, Aunt Louisa, it was nothing but a try for a pickup! He just wanted to—"

"Would you have been so aloof if it had been some young girl who'd spoken to you?"

"Why, I—"

"Look at him. A perfectly nice young man, casually but decently dressed. Just because he liked what he saw…and wanted to exchange a few words with you…"

Iris followed her aunt's gaze, and there he was, leaning against the doorway of the restaurant, looking over at them. When he saw their eyes on him he straightened up, looked expectant, and his lips curved up again.

When he smiled like that he was undeniably attractive. In fact, Iris thought, he was dazzling.

"I'm not in the habit of picking up gents in bars," Iris said stubbornly, and turned away. She was certainly astonished at her aunt's reaction. Of course she had brushed him off because he was a man! As he had singled her out because she was a girl. French, Italian, Spanish…you name it. Men were all the same. Always looking for a good thing.

"He…uh, doesn't give up easily," Louisa murmured. "Now he's come over and sat down. Two tables away from us."

"What should I do now, darling? Go over and throw my arms around him?"

This time a reproachful look came from her aunt. "Are we going to have a little spat just because, on our second day in Paris, my pretty niece made a conquest?"

"Certainly not, so forget about yon pushy gentleman and finish your coffee."

"I shall have *another* coffee," Louisa announced. "And so will you."

She looked about for the waiter, was unable to attract his attention, and in the next moment the persistent man a couple of tables away got up, strolled over to the white-jacketed waiter and pointed to the table where the two women sat.

"*Ah, oui,*" the waiter said briskly, and hurried over.

Then the man sat down again at his own table.

"*Oui, Madame?*" the waiter said to Louisa.

"Two more coffees, please."

"*Oui, oui, tout de suite,*" the waiter said, and rushed away.

"Thank you," Louisa called over to the other table.

"Not at all, Madame."

"If you're not expecting someone, would you care to join us?"

Without hesitation he rose, strolled over, and stood looking down at them. Then he pulled out a chair, said, "Madame, Mademoiselle," and sat down between them.

"It was kind of you to return my niece's travel folder," Louisa said.

"Not at all," he said again.

The waiter came back with their coffee.

"What will you have?" Louisa asked the newcomer.

"Thank you." He looked up at the waiter. *"Comme habitude,* Raoul," he said.

"Bon."

"What is that you asked for?" Louisa asked interestedly.

The man looked puzzled, then said, "Ah, I ordered coffee, but as I come here quite often for coffee I simply said, 'the usual,' and Raoul will bring me coffee."

"I must remember that idiom," Louisa said. *"Comme...?"*

"Comme habitude. Literally, 'as always.'"

When the coffee came he raised his cup and said, his glance encompassing them both, *"A votre santé."*

"You know that idiom," he commented, when Louisa, raising her own cup, answered him with, *"A le votre."*

And then, with a little bow, he added, "I am Paul Chandon."

"I'm Louisa Collinge and this is my niece Iris Easton."

He bowed again. "Madame...Mademoiselle. *Echanté.*"

So be it, Iris thought. After all, Aunt Louisa was the boss. And anyway, there was no harm in spending a few minutes with this young Frenchman. Perhaps her aunt was right. Maybe she had been a little brusque. Anyway, she was not alone, and if her aunt wished to palaver with the natives, it was her business.

"Monsieur Chandon told me he wants to improve his English," she told Louisa. "I can't imagine why. He speaks perfectly."

"Oh, no, many Gallicisms," Paul Chandon protested.

"I'm the one who should improve my French," Louisa said ruefully. "But like most Americans I'm a poor linguist. Henry spoke French very well."

"I see."

For a second Louisa looked a bit flustered. "My late husband," she explained hastily.

He turned to Iris. "When you spoke French to me, I admired very much your accent. You know how to say the R's."

"*Il fait beau aujourd'hui.*"

"Remarkable," he said politely. "What else besides the weather, Mademoiselle?"

Now, *that* sounds patronizing, Iris decided, annoyed, and gave him a level look. She would show this young boulevardier, this man who had nothing better to do with his time than loll about coffeehouses and try to pick up girls.

He sat waiting, his smile once again faintly amused, and Iris, stung, recited:

> *Dis, qu'as-tu fait, toi que voilá*
> *De ta jeuness?*

There was a charged silence, then he burst into laughter. Louisa looked mystified.

"What did you say?" she asked her niece. "It wasn't something off-color, was it?"

"Not off-color," Paul Chandon said, still laughing. "A bit impertinent, however."

"Well, what *was* it?"

"Your niece was quoting from Verlaine, the poet. She asked me, substantially, what have I done with my youth."

Louisa, looking disconcerted, gave Iris a questioning look, "I don't understand, what did you say to him?"

"It was just something from a famous poem," Iris murmured. "A random choice."

"Just the same," Paul Chandon remarked, "I will think twice before I ask you to speak French to me again."

"*Why?*" Louisa demanded, her eyes narrowing.

Her aunt looked really disturbed, Iris thought, and now rued her "random choice". She had more or less, in quoting that poem of a wastrel's despair, indicated that she thought *him* a prodigal and she saw that she would have to justify herself in her aunt's eyes.

"You see," she said, gesturing helplessly, "it's just so embarrassing when someone asks for an impromptu chat in a foreign language. So I just fell back on…on poetry."

She was talking fast now, and only for her aunt's benefit. She didn't give a hoot what this bon vivant thought about her, and if he was insulted, so much the better.

"I *love* Verlaine," she said vehemently. "And everyone knows that verse."

"*I* don't," Louisa said pointedly.

"Then I must give you a book of Verlaine's poems for your birthday."

"I can't read French, not any longer. So don't waste your money. It's just that I don't understand about this "youth" business. What was it you said? Only tell me in English."

"I will," Paul said, seeming not at all put out but instead highly entertained. "It goes like this: 'You there…what have you done with your young days?'"

A little puzzled, as if the whole thing was over her head, Louisa finally shrugged. "Since you're just a young man, Paul, the poem can't apply in any way to you."

She sipped her coffee.

"Then why did it strike you that way?" she demanded.

He visibly controlled a smile. For a second his eyes met Iris's. Then he said, very seriously, "Perhaps it does apply to me…in a way."

And before Louisa could say anything more on the subject, he drained his coffee cup and made a suggestion.

"There's a slight chill in the air today. Shall we have a cognac?"

"Not for me," Iris said.

"Oh, do have one, I'm going to," Louisa urged.

Now it was Iris who looked at her watch. "Don't you think we had better be going, Auntie? We can't waste too much time, and besides going to Notre Dame, you said we'd have lunch on the Ile St. Louis."

"Lunch on the Ile? That's a splendid idea," Paul said. "I know a restaurant…a bistro, on the Ile St. Louis which I think you would like. Very Parisian, not fancy, you understand, and not generally known to Americans, who generally seek out more elegant surroundings."

"Not these Americans," Iris retorted, nettled. "That's why we're staying at the Vendôme, whereas the kind of Americans you're speaking of gravitate to the Ritz or the Crillon."

"I see," he answered.

She gave him a sidelong glance. Did his eyes look amused? Was he laughing at her?

"It does occur to me," he said gravely, "that the Hotel Vendôme is considered—certainly by me and my friends—to have its own quiet distinction."

He called over the man who had been waiting on them. "Raoul?"

The man came over. "Will it be three cognacs?" Paul asked Iris.

"None for me, thanks," she said.

"*Deux cognacs*, then, Raoul."

"*Merci mon vieux.*"

When the liqueurs came, there was a repetition of the "to your health" toast and then Paul held the small glass to his nose for a second or two.

Finally he drained it all in one gulp.

Good, now we can go, Iris thought, itching to get on with the day's sightseeing. But her aunt, leaning back comfortably in her chair, sipped her drink slowly and pulled a cigarette out of her purse.

Paul flicked a lighter for her and then said, "You won't mind if I smoke, then?"

"Good heavens, why should I? Have you been refraining out of politeness?"

"Certainly. It's very little to ask."

"That's what I most admire about you Europeans, you young ones. Respect and courtesy are sadly lacking in America. Young people there are too often rude, crude and uncouth."

She cast a fond glance at her niece. "But not Iris," she said, with pride. "It's not often I find fault with her behavior."

"And when you do you tell me so in no uncertain terms," Iris remarked.

"Of course. I want you to be perfect."

"One can see that this young lady is, as you say in your country, the apple of your eye, Madame," Paul murmured and, with a little bow to Iris, said something in French.

> *"'Nous sommes les Ingénues*
> *Aux bandeaux plats, à l'oeil bleu…'"*

"What does it mean?" Louisa asked. "Do you know what it means, Iris?"

Flushed, Iris looked away. What Paul Chandon had said was easily translated. And he had paid her back. In the same way she had rebuffed him, he had rebuffed her.

Very cleverly, too. Paul Chandon had retaliated in kind: he had quoted the same poet, Verlaine.

Flushing, furious, the words he had said rang in her mind.

> 'Ingenues, not quite grown
> Blue-eyed, braids around the head…'

So he thought her an ingenue, did he? "Oh, do tell me," Louisa cried. "What did he *say?*"

"Something about young blue-eyed girls," Iris said stiffly.

"So you see, Mademoiselle," Paul murmured, "it doesn't apply to you, and was simply a random choice."

She looked directly at him, her eyes hot and angry. "I understand," she said slowly. "And now that we're even, we really must go, I'm afraid. That is, if you're quite ready, Aunt Louisa."

Paul held up a hand for their waiter, who came over.

"*L'addition, s'il vous plait.*"

When the man had scribbled some hen tracks on his pad, he tore the sheet off and handed it to Paul. But Louisa calmly pulled the check out of his hand.

"Madame, if you please," Paul protested.

Louisa just smiled, pulled out some paper money from her alligator handbag and put it on the little tray. Then she fished for some coins and threw them carelessly on the small heap.

Paul chuckled, stayed the waiter's eager hand, and scraped up two of the coins, pushing them back toward Louisa.

"Better luck next time, Raoul," he said to the waiter, who shrugged, grinned and picked up the rest of the money.

"You left too much for the service," Paul said chidingly. "You will spoil them for us Parisians. Americans are very generous, but the French will not thank you for overtipping."

"I just can't help it," Louisa said, sighing. "I'm so used to a minimum of twenty percent."

Iris stood up, her tote bag and camera all ready over her shoulder. She was not exactly tapping her foot, but she did want to get on with it.

It earned her another odd look from her aunt. Disapproving, but something else besides…somewhat conjecturing, somewhat reflective. And as if to punish her niece for her unseemly show of haste, she took her own sweet time in gathering her belongings together.

When she did get up, she seemed to consider a moment or two and then, apparently making up her mind, faced Paul Chandon with a question.

"I suppose you're busy and must rush away somewhere, Paul?"

He shrugged.

"Not at all, Madame. This is too nice a day to pay much attention to tiresome duties. As a matter of fact, I rather wanted to guide you over to the little bistro on the Ile St. Louis. The one I told you about."

"I wouldn't want to impose," Louisa said, but she looked delighted.

Iris, unable to hide her annoyance any longer, put in an objection. "Isn't it a bit early for lunch? And as I recall, we were going to the cathedral."

Her aunt and Paul regarded her simultaneously. Her aunt with a frankly irritable expression, Paul with grave speculation. She was totally exasperated with the status quo, and at the same time felt like a fractious child, particularly when Paul and her aunt left off looking at her and turned to each other silently.

There was a long, uncomfortable interval which Iris herself at last broke.

"I seem to be not quite myself," she said, the words coming out in a kind of staccato. "I'll do whatever you like."

"Are you ill, perhaps?" her aunt asked.

"No, *no!*"

"It *is* early for lunch," Louisa finally said. "Yet I'd dearly love to have it in that little bistro our friend has been telling us about. Can we go to Notre Dame first, then? And afterwards to the Ile St. Louis…would that be all right with everyone?"

"If you are sure that…" Paul began.

"Iris?" her aunt demanded implacably.

There was nothing to do but answer, with as agreeable a smile as she could muster, "All right with me. Yes, fine."

They started walking, heading for the Pont St. Michel.

And instead of positioning himself between the two women, as would have been expected, Paul walked on the other side of Louisa, so that his comments were directed to her, rather than to both of them.

They crossed the bridge over the Seine, Louisa pausing in the center of it to give a loving, comprehensive glance at the beautiful panorama spread out before them.

On the other side, Paul pointed. "The Palais de Justice," he said. "And just ahead, as you can see, Notre Dame."

Iris forgot about everything else. Nothing could mar her awe and reverence. The great Gothic cathedral, with its twin towers and the lofty spire at the center of the apse, sent her into a transport.

The cathedral of Notre Dame…

"Here," Paul said, as they drew nearer to it, "is the great square which is so famous in fiction. Victor Hugo. You have read *The Hunchback of Notre* Dame?"

"Of course," Iris said impatiently.

"This is where Quasimodo was scourged, and where Esmeralda gave him to drink."

"Charles Laughton was so splendid in that part," Louisa said. "They simply don't make films like that any more."

"But the book was better," Iris commented ironically.

"It's so long since I read it."

"And I too," Paul said, chuckling. "I am getting on in years, I'm afraid, as I was so recently reminded."

He was looking at Iris, but she declined to return his smiling glance. They went up the long flight of steps, worn with the tread of centuries of feet that had climbed the ancient stone, and then on into the great Gothic cathedral that was, almost certainly, the most venerated house of worship in the world.

After that, everything else was forgotten. Everything but the vast edifice itself, and in the silence that was broken only by an occasional footfall, time seemed to come to a stop, earthly matters fall away.

In this place one truly felt alone, Iris thought…alone with history and with God. Scarcely knowing that she had left the others behind, she wandered off by herself, absorbed in a transcendental reverie that took her far away from the present and into the long-gone past.

Five

As she left the cathedral, Iris looked about for her aunt, wandering slowly through the narrow side aisles, her eyes searching for Louisa.

There were few people visiting Notre Dame at this hour of the day. Most were lunching somewhere, or sitting outside in the sun. There was no sign of either her aunt or Paul Chandon, so they must, Iris realized, have had their fill of the beauty in this place of solemn grandeur and left her to sate herself alone. After all, both of them had been here many, many times.

With a last, lingering look at the great rose windows she went through the huge, parted doors that had welcomed so many people for so many years. Then, blinking in the sudden brightness after the time spent in the shadowy confines within, stepped back a bit.

She was groping in her tote bag for her sunglasses when she caught sight of them. There was her aunt, standing in the great square outside, and there was Paul Chandon beside her. They were at some distance and looked, like the others down below, slightly in miniature.

They also looked as if they were very much enjoying each other's company. Iris watched them curiously. From where she stood, her aunt looked incredibly youthful, with her trim figure and slim, pretty legs. Several inches shorter than her companion, her face turned up as she spoke animatedly to him, she presented a most attractive picture.

For a second or two longer Iris, unobserved, regarded the two. Now her aunt had lifted a hand to smooth away a strand of hair the wind had blown across her forehead. With a gallant gesture, Paul Chandon reached down and brushed another strand away.

An imaginary strand, Iris told herself irritably...and an exaggeratedly gallant gesture.

Why, he's not going to "guide" us to that bistro on the Ile St. Louis, she thought. He had no intention of showing them the place and then bowing out of the picture. He would wheedle her aunt into invitation. They were probably talking about it right this minute!

"Of course you'll join us for lunch," Louisa would say cordially.

Well, why not?

Because he's spoiling everything, Iris thought vexedly. He was pushy and arrogant and who was he, anyway? Someone they knew nothing about, idling his days away.

What did he do for a living, if anything? Why was he bumming about on a weekday, instead of being in an office somewhere?

If he was on vacation, what was he doing in Paris, where he obviously lived? If he were on vacation, he'd be somewhere else… not here, in the city.

"I am Paul Chandon…"

That was all he had said about himself.

Why in the world was Aunt Louisa behaving in this foolhardy manner?

There was only one explanation. Her aunt was encouraging this stranger because he had made a play for her niece, and Aunt Louisa had some insane notion that here, like manna from heaven, was a handsome and "presentable" young man for her niece to have a few dates with…and all without any blame to herself for having introduced him to Iris.

I can handle this, Iris decided grimly, and set her lips. Then she went down the steps. They saw her finally, as she came toward them.

"Here she is," Louisa said gaily, and as Iris walked up to them, added, "You will join us for lunch, Paul, won't you?"

"I only meant to show you where the restaurant was," he reminded her, and then shrugged engagingly. "However, I haven't eaten yet either, so thank you very much, I would like to."

I knew it, thought Iris…I knew it…

The Ile St. Louis was reached by going round to the side of the cathedral where there was a paradise of beautiful gardens and where people sat on white-painted benches, their faces turned up to the sun, and small children played.

"I'm so fond of this spot," Louisa said. "Isn't it idyllic, Iris? The trees, the foliage, the fragrances…"

"It's a good place in which to sit with a book and read for an afternoon," Paul suggested. His eyes followed Iris's as she looked up at the massive flying buttresses that flanked the cathedral.

"That's inspiring too, isn't it," he said. "A place in which to put aside worldly cares."

He looked back at her quizzically.

"And in which to forget minor irritations," he added. Then, putting a hand briefly on her arm, met her eyes.

"Are you," he asked, "feeling more serene now? After your long session in the church?"

She flushed angrily. It was as if he had said, *are you more resigned to my unwelcome presence?*

I would like, Iris thought, to see you fall, fully clad, into the Seine. Or simply vanish in a puff of smoke.

But she gritted her teeth and smiled. "How could anyone feel anything but serene on a day like this?"

"I am glad," he said, with that faintly sardonic smile, and turned back to her aunt.

Finally they came to a small chain-fence gate, which Paul opened. They went through it and stepped onto a quaint little iron bridge, which spanned the river at this narrow point. And then they were on the Ile St. Louis, which was almost like a little tail of the Ile de la Cité where Notre Dame stood.

It was very pretty, with its tree-lined embankments. Paul led them down a narrow street and then into a narrower one where, among three or four restaurants, was a corner one.

"Et voilá," he said. *"Le Coquelicot."*

It was, as he had told them, far from fancy, and when they were seated, Louisa admitted that she would certainly have passed this place by, as it looked from the outside like a Greasy Spoon.

Modest in appearance, it was not a tourist place, probably due to its unprepossessing exterior which was undoubtedly designed in order to ensure strictly a French clientele.

There was, at least today, not a single person of another nationality present save for Iris and her aunt, and the sound of many Gallic voices raised in talk and laughter was diverting. Typically bistro, there were the usual red-checked cloths spread over wood trestle tables. The chairs were rush-bottomed and there was a rough-beamed ceiling.

A waiter came over and greeted them. To Paul, he said, *"Ça va, mon gosse,"* and handed him three menus.

His eyes assessed the two people with Paul, lingering first on Iris, then Louisa, and then returning to Paul.

Iris caught the quick exchange of looks between Paul and the waiter. She felt uncomfortable and uneasy. It was as if they were being sized up for some reason.

The waiter, with a pleasant smile, left them to make their selections.

"I'm starved," Louisa said. "I'll have the choucroute."

"What's that?" Iris wanted to know.

Paul explained. "Slabs of pork, with beans, sauerkraut, and a frankfurter."

"I guess I'll have that too."

When the waiter returned Paul gave the order for three choucroutes and a bottle of *vin ordinaire.*

"Ah, *pain riche,*" Louisa said contentedly, reaching in a wicker bread basket. "Try it, Iris, it's delicious."

The bread, spread with sweet butter of which there was a generous crock, was certainly very tasty. "I do like this bistro,"

Louisa said enthusiastically, "though I doubt I'd come in by myself…that is, without someone French. I'd feel out of place."

"You wouldn't now," Paul assured her. "Now you are known here, and will always be a welcome guest."

"You do seem to know all the waiters in Paris," Iris commented.

"Only the ones at the eating places to which I go," he replied, with a perfectly straight face.

"How amusing," she said sweetly.

He leaned across the table.

"Permit me," he said, politely, and brushed her chin lightly with a corner of his red-checked napkin. "You had a crumb of bread on your face."

"Thank you."

"Not at all."

Iris felt the color rise to her cheeks. She was irritated beyond words at the hot flush that seemed to actually burn…and doubly irked that it was not so much flush as blush, that she was blushing, like a silly girl, a goose.

She caught her aunt's eye and thought she saw a flicker of amusement there, a faint look of speculative merriment. For one awful moment there were tears very near the surface.

What was the matter with her?

Then she was herself again, almost instantly. It was the unfamiliar, the new, that was all. Maybe a little homesickness. She was perhaps jealous too. Jealous of Paul Chandon, who had so captivated her aunt. She wasn't accustomed to sharing Louisa's affections.

"I'd like some more of that butter," she said, without a trace of tremor in her voice.

"And here is our lunch," Paul announced, replacing his napkin on his lap as three steaming plates of food were set before them.

"*Bon,*" Paul said, and all the glasses were filled.

The waiter, with a "*Bon appétit,*" hurried away.

Louisa, fork poised, gave a happy little sigh. "'A loaf of bread, a jug of wine…'"

"And thou," Paul finished for her. He raised his glass. *"Bonne chance et bon destin."*

There wasn't much to do except raise one's own glass and drink to the toast. If only he wouldn't *smile* like that, Iris thought, averting her eyes quickly. That smile, so warm and dazzling…it seemed so sincere. Whereas, he was not sincere. He was out for something, he had something up his sleeve. He was an adventurer, up to no good, and she was a captive, fated to follow her aunt's whims.

It was all very perplexing…and very worrisome.

But the choucroute was succulent and tasty, and the wine a little heady. It seemed innocent enough, but it had a kick all right, and they hadn't had a bite to eat since breakfast.

"Dessert?" Louisa cried, when Paul asked what they would like for a sweet. "I'm stuffed. Absolutely not."

"Nor I," Iris said.

"I also am *rassasier,*" he admitted. "But please, ladies, not to use that expression even if I did, as it is somewhat vulgar."

"It probably means stuffed," Louisa said, laughing, "which is not exactly acceptable in polite society. But I will have a demi tasse and Iris, you will too, I suppose."

"Yes, please."

"I'll attend to it," Paul said, and rose with a murmured, *"Pardon…"*

Louisa's eyes followed him with, Iris thought, an admiring look. "Isn't he nice," she murmured. "And this is really a fun place to eat. Henry and I had our favorite dining spots here on the Ile. I guess I'll bypass them, this trip at least. I am *so* glad to have you with me. I don't suppose you can possibly know how much it means."

"Which is a nice way of saying that I'm doing you a favor by being here," Iris said gently. "You're a dear aunt and a dear person." She leaned forward. "You know how I feel about you," she continued earnestly. "But darling, you mustn't try to…you know you promised that…"

"Yes, dear?"

But there was no time. She heard the approaching footsteps. Paul, returning, slid into his chair again. He reached in his shirt pocket and pulled out a packet of cigarettes.

"Madame," he said, offering it first to Louisa.

"Thank you."

"Mademoiselle?"

"No, thanks."

Their coffee came and the waiter went off again. The sun, strong and beneficent, shone through the mullioned window, and the crowd inside began to thin out. Soon there were only three tables occupied, their own and two others.

"More coffee?" Paul asked.

"No. We must go, I'm afraid. I'm sorry too. It's been so nice. Paul, would you get our waiter, please?"

He came over. *"Oui, Madame?"*

"Our check, please."

He shook his head. *"Pas aujourd'hui, Madame."*

Louisa turned to Paul. "What does he say?"

"Apparently it's on the house," Paul replied, with a faint shrug.

She stared at the waiter, and then back at Paul. "So that was why you excused yourself," she cried. "You took care of the bill, didn't you?"

But she didn't make an issue of it, simply said, "Then next time, Paul, you will be *my* guest. That is, if there will be a next time?"

"I would be most unhappy if there were to be no next time," he said gravely.

"I'm glad. Then thank you for this very good meal and for introducing me to this charming little place. And if you can suggest an evening for us to have dinner together, I'd be pleased."

"Would tomorrow evening suit you, Madame?"

"That would be splendid."

No one consults me, Iris thought. And so it was to be a steady threesome. She was beside herself with alarm. This was simply not to be believed! This utter stranger…who knew what his reputation was?

Her aunt's face, radiant and happy, appalled her. Why, she looked as anticipative as a young girl on the eve of her first prom…as if…

An unpleasant thought came to her, unpleasant and unwelcome…but gaining momentum. A thought that had leapt up at her suddenly and horribly…

There, she thought, was this affluent-looking woman, her aunt. Marvelous clothes, chic hairdo, carefully manicured nails. Why, that alligator handbag alone was worth a few hundred dollars… and the gold jewelry, the chain round her neck, the bracelets, the rings…

And on the other side, this suave young man, with his practiced charm, his dazzling smile…

Louisa, in her mid-forties, was an attractive, even alluring woman, a woman no man—even someone Paul Chandon's age— would be ashamed to be seen with.

How often had she heard her aunt say, "Women of middle age are far better off in Europe than in the United States. They're not written off as dull and dreary, or physically undesirable. Rather, their status improves. Europeans appreciate women with experience and savoir faire."

Those words came back to Iris now. Experience and savoir faire…

Some other words, so recently voiced, echoed in her mind as well.

"'Ingenues, not quite grown…'"

In other words, inexperienced girls without savoir faire…like herself.

Who was this Paul Chandon pursuing, when it came right down to it? Iris Easton…or Louisa Collinge?

Once again her face flooded with color, followed by a wave of angry, wry consternation and the feeling that someone had punched her in the stomach. She had been so sure that he was eyeing her, Iris, as a promising possibility.

But instead, couldn't it be her aunt he was contemplating as a soft touch?

A woman, for example, who could well, very well, afford to stay at the Ritz but instead preferred the Vendôme…which, according to Paul Chandon, had its own "quiet distinction."

A woman who was far from old, much more than merely goodlooking to boot, and who clearly had a lot of money.

Why, that's the way it was! Not what she had thought…no, not at all. Paul Chandon wasn't one bit interested in the niece. He was interested—and very much so—in the aunt.

And the way Louisa catered to him.

My God, Iris thought…where would this lead?

Her aunt's voice came to her, as if from a great distance. With difficulty she tore herself away from a horrid fantasy.

"Yes?"

"Paul asked where we would like to dine tomorrow evening."

"Why don't we ask Paul to make one of his interesting suggestions?" Iris said brightly. "Since I know nothing about restaurants here, and he obviously knows a great deal, wouldn't it be logical to rely on his vast experience?"

He seemed not to notice the bite in her words. He only nodded, turned to Louisa and asked if she had a preference. When she said no, he nodded agreeably, and told her he would select a restaurant that might be new to her despite the fact that she was no stranger to Paris.

"We'll look forward to it," Louisa said, with a soft smile. Her uptilted eyes, green today because she was wearing a suit of that color, were luminous.

Iris looked away. She was sickened, positively sickened, by the glow on her aunt's face.

No fool like an old fool, she thought, was instantly contrite, but saw no real reason to amend her harsh judgment.

Oh, poor Aunt Louisa! Lonely, grief-crazed; Henryless…and seizing on the first young Frenchman who gave her the glad eye.

She had visions of cabling home to her parents.

Aunt Louisa in danger of being victimized by a fortune-hunter. What shall I do?

As if they could help! As if anyone could.

It's up to me, Iris thought anxiously, to discourage this cheeky young man in every way I can.

At the moment, however, the problem seemed somewhat insoluble.

Six

When they left the bistro, Louisa suggested that they take a walk along one of the quays on the Ile St. Louis. "The Quai d'Orléans is my favorite. How about you, Paul?"

"My favorite too," he agreed.

They turned left, then right and were soon wending their way along a riverside street that was almost miraculously beautiful. The trees that bordered the embankment leaned toward the river, with some of the branches actually touching the water. There was a sense of being in another age, another era and Iris wouldn't have been at all surprised to see someone come out of any one of the handsome old houses that lined the street, dressed in Empire clothing…or glimpse a horse-drawn fiacre just up ahead.

No one, however, came out of any of the houses, nor was anyone, save for themselves, in sight. The long, winding quay was deserted, hushed…like a dream vista.

In spite of Iris's recent consternation, she was unable to feel anything but euphoric on this peaceful quay and, taking out her camera, shot almost half a roll of film. To the right, where Notre Dame presented itself from the rear, and from which angle it was even more grand and thrilling than from its front facade, the scene was incomparable.

The Seine, seen from this vantage point, with those magnificent trees shadowing it and the water craft, like little toys moving leisurely across its green-blue surface, was like a poem.

"The quays of the Ile St. Louis are best in the very early morning," Paul said, when Iris at last put her camera away. "In the hours after dawn there is a faint, rather mysterious haze that shadows everything…as if a fine veil of gauze had been drawn over the environs. No one is about then, except for a young boy on his bicycle delivering the morning papers."

"No one's about now," Iris commented. "Only us."

"True…but in the time of day I speak of, it is as if no one would ever be about…as if…"

He broke off a little self-consciously. "I talk too much," he said. "And often about ridiculous things."

For a split second Iris wanted to like this man because of what he had just said. She had the oddest feeling that he had been going to finish his sentence with the words "as if there were no one but oneself in the whole world."

It was a feeling she herself knew, felt occasionally. That, on some quiet and unpeopled street, she was absolutely alone, and that everyone else had either died or never been born. And she was on her own, forevermore, without help, company or the voices of others.

"Well," Paul said briskly, "now that you have seen something of the Ile. St. Louis, what about St. Germain? All tourists want to go there, mainly to take snapshots of themselves at *Deux Magots.*"

The moment of tentative rapport, in which Iris had been unexpectedly drawn to the man who was looking down at her, died with a dull thud. Antipathy returned and, with it, the determination not to be fooled by him again. There was simply nothing about this Paul Chandon that was of any merit and she would somehow convince her aunt that he was up to no good. He said these nasty things to upset her, that was the size of it. And just when she had thought there might be some decency in him. Of *course* she wanted to go to St. Germain and of *course* she wanted to go to the celebrated cafe called *Deux Magots.* But she was *not* every tourist, she was not some American hick who said ooh la la, thought the Folies Bergère was the height of sophistication and Maxim's the last word in culinary splendor. She was an educated girl of good family and how *dare* he presume anything about her?

"We can walk there," Louisa said, approving of the suggestion.

"Is that okay with you, Mademoiselle?" Paul asked politely.

She flinched at the American slang, which she was sure had been to bring the conversation down to what he considered her level…that of 'an ingenue, not quite grown.' In other words, she thought furiously, wet behind the ears.

I dislike this man intensely, she told herself, and answered curtly, "Okay with me," emphasizing the 'okay' with elaborate irony.

He simply laughed, moved to her aunt's right and, as before, there was Louisa in the middle, with the two younger people on either side of her.

At least I don't have to look at him or listen to his insolent remarks, Iris thought. He and her aunt were carrying on their own sprightly chitchat, most of which was lost to Iris because of the brisk breeze that blew his words away.

Better so, she felt crossly, and turned her attention to the beauties spread out before her.

They retraced their steps, going over the iron bridge to the Ile de la Cité again, walked back through the gardens to the front of the cathedral, and crossed back to the Left Bank on the Pont St. Michel.

This brought them back to the cafe in which they had met earlier. If only they hadn't stopped here those few hours ago, Iris thought, this persistent stranger wouldn't be with them now, holding her aunt's arm and sticking to them like glue.

Or like a leech, more likely…

If only they hadn't stopped here.

They didn't stop here now, at any rate, but continued on past the Place St. Michel, Paul saying, "Now we are on the Boul' Mich', on our way to St. Germain, but first we will go a little farther so that you can have a look at the Sorbonne where a hundred years ago I was attending my lectures."

Another dig at me, Iris thought, and avoided his teasing glance at her.

"There's the Cluny Museum," Louisa told her, at the junction where the Boul' Mich' crossed with the Boulevard St. Germain. "You might want to go there sometime."

After that the area became very noisy and cluttered, with students coming and going, clustering in groups, and the sprawl of the Sorbonne acting as a backdrop. The dome of the Panthéon rose behind it.

There was a variety of eating places, all piled up side by side in a kind of jumble, with the smell of food and the redolence of Gauloise cigarettes spicing the air.

A group of four young people, standing outside of one of the cafes, was engaged in what appeared to be quite serious talk. They didn't look giddy, or infantilely inconsequential. They looked, in fact, like kids you'd want to know.

Iris rather imagined that they were discussing politics or something like the Common Market. Most of the students, in fact, had the air of being preoccupied with things other than drugs, sex or gay liberation…or at least not obsessed with them.

One young couple, walking close together, drew Iris's attention particularly. Both were in jeans, sloppy shirts and zori sandals. The boy, who was only a shade taller than his girl, had a pally arm slung over her shoulder.

They probably lived together, showered together, and would very possibly go separate ways when the semester was over. But that affectionate arm slung over the shoulder of the girl, and their carefree camaraderie…it was somehow so…so touching.

They finally disappeared into one of the restaurants, but Iris kept thinking about them and when Paul said, "Lively place, isn't it?" she answered abstractedly, "Uh huh."

"If we continued on," he told her, "we would come to the Place Edmond Rostand. You know *Cyrano de Bergerac,* Mademoiselle?"

"I have a nodding acquaintance with it," she answered shortly.

His faintly amused smile came at that, and she turned away.

Then they walked back to the Boulevard St. Germain and veered toward the left.

These exquisite, broad boulevards were so gorgeous, Iris mused, and one of the many bonanzas of the city—spacious, rich in trees whose sturdy trunks and great spreading branches provided shady oases. The buildings themselves were a joy to stare at. Handsome and finely-wrought, with their massive doors adorned with wonderful carvings and highly-polished brasses, each one seemed more magnificent than the other.

New York was, admittedly, a glittering city, with its towers of glass and steel, its fine shops, art galleries and museums. But in New York there was much visible evidence of rot and decay, so much ugliness mixed with the splendor. Further, you never saw the sky in New York, only bits and pieces of it. The tall buildings swallowed it up.

It was the sky here, the great, astonishing sweep of it always and ineluctably part of the landscape, that enthralled one so.

After a while they came to the small square where the church of St. Germain was located. L'église de Saint-Germain-des-Près was the oldest church in Paris. Small, rough-hewn as to stone, it had a simple, countrified air, looking like almost any village church in provincial districts, which, of course, in times long gone, it had been.

And there, just across the square, was the famed *Deux Magots*, with its green canopy lettered in pseudo Chinese characters and its clutter of round white tables massed in the outside area…most of which were occupied.

They found a table with only two chairs, but in a short time Paul had rounded up another one. He sat down, stretched out his long legs and said, "Now you are in Existentialist territory, Mademoiselle."

Iris refrained from comment. As if she didn't know that! Next he would inform her, in arrogant, pontifical manner, that Jean Paul Sartre and Simone de Beauvoir had given the vicinity its present popularity with the intellectuals. Present her with a little lesson in past and present history.

She was silent, feeling that if she uttered one word, she would start to sputter. When the coffee they had ordered was brought to the table, she had an almost unconquerable compulsion to throw the contents of her cup right in his face.

She got up quickly, with her camera. Instantly, Paul smiled knowingly and said, "Be sure you get the canopy in your picture."

She turned sharply away and focused on the church.

Photographing it from several angles, she took some other snaps of the surroundings. When she glanced back at their table, neither Paul nor her aunt noticed, so she quickly snapped a picture of the cafe, careful to get the canopy with its sign in proper range.

Fooled him, the smart aleck, she thought and, reaching in her tote bag, pulled out her Paris map.

She found the spot where they were now and thus oriented herself. Here they were, at this square, and up the street was the Rue Bonaparte, where the ecole des Beaux-Arts was located. On the other side of the Boulevard St. Germain was the Rue de Rennes, crisscrossing with the Boulevard Raspail…which she had so often run across in reading Balzac.

She put the map away and looked across to where her aunt and Paul Chandon were sitting. They were deep in conversation. Louisa was leaning back in her chair: Paul, with both elbows on the table, seemed to be saying something very confidential. Both faces were serious and reflective.

And again it struck Iris that Louisa was an unmistakably attractive woman, besides being rich as well.

Just then both looked up, as if they had felt Iris's prolonged study of them, and Louisa waved. Reluctantly Iris walked back, but before she could sit down her aunt suggested that they take some "people" pictures.

"We must have some shots of ourselves," she said gaily. "Iris, why don't you take one of Paul and me, and then I'll take one of you and Paul."

There was nothing to do but comply. "Ready?" Iris prompted, and snapped the picture. Then, of course, her aunt got up and Iris had to pose with Paul.

"You're too far away from each other," Louisa complained. "One of you move a bit. That's better. Now how about a lovely smile, Iris?"

After that Paul in turn took a picture of aunt and niece.

"I don't know where the time has gone, but it's four-thirty," Louisa said soon after they had finished their second coffees. "Iris, unless you want to go back by cab, we have a long walk before we're home again."

"I'd love to walk, but you must be rather tired by now. Don't you think we'd better take a taxi?"

It was mean of her to underline the fact that her aunt was old enough to tire more easily than someone younger, but she couldn't help herself. Someone had to save Aunt Louisa from making a Big Mistake. Her aunt really must take into account that this eager stranger was a good fifteen years younger than she was.

But it fell on deaf ears. Louisa, holding up a mirror from her purse, went on serenely applying lipstick.

"One expects to get tired when traveling," she said, dropping lipstick and mirror into her alligator handbag and then giving a little stretch.

And if Iris had any idea that now they would go their way and Paul Chandon would go his, she was sadly mistaken. Nothing was said in her hearing, but it had apparently been agreed that he would accompany them back to their hotel.

It was, however, a shorter walk this time. They cut over to the Quai Voltaire and crossed to the Right Bank by means of the Pont Royal, and were at the Concorde before Iris realized it.

And then the hotel was more or less right around the corner.

"I have so much enjoyed this," Paul said when he left them just outside the Vendôme. "It was the most delightful day I have had in a very long time."

He picked up Louisa's right hand and kissed it. But for Iris there was merely a brush of the lips on her own hand…then he quickly relinquished it.

Nevertheless her hand tingled and, why it was that she felt a quick thrill at the contact, she couldn't have said. Since this questionable stranger was so antipathetic to her, the unbidden response was puzzling.

When they were upstairs and in the salon again, Louisa kicked off her shoes even before she sat down on the sofa. "How good that feels," she sighed. "Well, darling, did you have a super day?"

"Super and then some. Except that—"

A telephone shrilled in Louisa's room.

"Why don't you go inside and rest a bit before dinner," her aunt suggested to Iris. "I know I'm going to, just as soon as I see who that is on the phone."

So Iris's objections about Paul Chandon had to be tabled.

And in her room, stretched out on the comfy bed, she thought that, in any event, what *could* she say that would be delicate and tactful? She might just say all the wrong things and, instead of ameliorating the situation, might push her aunt in the wrong direction. Louisa, annoyed and hurt, might be more of a ready prey for Chandon.

It was all very difficult, and it was giving her a headache.

They had dinner at a restuarant only a block or so away from the hotel, the King Charles, where the onion soup was worth a Pindaric ode. It was not a "chichi" place, Louisa pointed out, but the cuisine was unfailingly good and the restaurant itself handy to the hotel.

Nor did they linger. They were back in their rooms a scant hour later. Over a nightcap of some Courvoisier Louisa had bought in the bar downstairs, they both agreed they would read in bed for a while and then, as Iris put it, "pack it in."

But when she was alone in her bedroom, Iris made only a half-hearted attempt at reading. The words blurred on the page and she kept wondering if her aunt was thinking, perhaps fatuously, about that dreadful Paul Chandon.

Would it, perhaps, be better for Louisa to be thinking about Paul Chandon than lying in bed missing her dead husband?

Not once had her aunt shown distress at being in Paris, the city she claimed to love more than any other, without Uncle Henry at her side. No tears, no long face…and yet it must be very painful for her.

Would a small flirtation with a younger man really be of any harm, after all?

But why would this much younger man be agreeable to such a thing? Unless it meant something in his pocket.

He *has* to be a scrounger, Iris decided, hardening her heart once more, and rubbing hard at her hand, where the feel of that man's lips against it still tingled.

Seven

It was the sun that woke Iris early the next morning, for she had neglected to pull the drapes the night before. Shafts of it rayed through the high windows, tracing golden patterns on the carpet.

It was only six-thirty, but she didn't go back to sleep. She was for some reason—and glad of it—in a much, much better mood than the night before. She had been silly about the events of yesterday, really silly. Nothing at all had happened: they had simply met a man who for some reason her aunt had taken a passing fancy to and whom Iris herself had felt just the opposite about.

They were seeing him for dinner tonight, true…but in the meantime Louisa had enjoyed yesterday with him and this evening would probably be bored to tears…and that would be the end of that.

She went to the desk, took some stationery from the drawer, and wrote a long, enthusiastic letter to her parents, describing, in rather purple prose, the glories of the city. She also wrote one to Jeff and, besides those, half a dozen postcards.

Then it was time to shower and dress.

The salon, bright and cheerful as always in the limpid light of a Paris morning, was heartening. Louisa was already there, sitting on the Recamier sofa and doing something she rarely was guilty of…smoking a pre-breakfast cigarette.

Iris knew instantly that something was troubling her aunt. It was the cigarette at this early hour, and something else too…a a discontented, even downcast look on Louisa's face.

"I've called down," she said, in a kind of curt way. "Breakfast will be here soon."

"How did you sleep?"

"So so. You?"

"Marvelously. Nothing like walking your legs off to give you a good night's snooze."

A knock came at the door. *"Entrez,"* Louisa called, and the young waiter who served them each morning wheeled in their tray.

"Bonjour," he said, with his shy smile.

"Bonjour, Matthieu."

He put the tray on the coffee table and then wheeled out the cart.

"Have you anything planned for today?" Iris asked, as her aunt poured their coffee.

Her aunt, Iris couldn't help noticing, ate listlessly, crumbling her croissant with distracted fingers. What could be wrong with her?

She didn't find out until they had collected their cameras and handbags for the day's sightseeing. It was when Iris commented that they would have to plan their points of interest carefully because of their appointment with Paul Chandon in the evening that Iris learned what it was that was bugging her aunt.

"Oh," Louisa said. "I'm sorry, I forgot to tell you. He called this morning and begged off. Something came up, he said, and he won't be able to make it."

So that was why Louisa was so distraught.

It was with a mixture of feelings that Iris gave a quick look at her aunt's face and then just as quickly looked away.

Why, Aunt Louisa was definitely, decidedly, upset about the whole thing! Not only that, but something seemed to have gone out of her…she looked deflated, pale, and…and really miserable.

I just don't understand it, Iris thought unhappily. How could she have been so swiftly, and unmistakably, captivated by that man? Aunt Louisa? *Her* Aunt Louisa?

What could one make of it? she wondered and then, perversely, she herself was miffed. It was a rejection, after all, and reflected on her as well. Probably he had decided that it would be too difficult to shake off the niece in order to concentrate on the aunt.

Good riddance, she decided. And now they wouldn't have to think about time. They could have another long, blissful day all by themselves.

Just the same, some of her aunt's malaise had rubbed off on her and like Louisa, Iris couldn't seem to shake off the crossness with which she started their day's junket.

Furthermore, it quickly became clear that whatever she wanted to do would have to be outlined by herself. Louisa was abstracted, and even a bit short of temper.

"Today would be a good day to go to the Champs de Mars," Iris proposed. "After all, I've only seen the top of the Eiffel Tower from a great distance."

"You haven't even been *inside* the Louvre," her aunt said querulously. "Don't you think that's a little bit ridiculous?"

"I just thought we could save it for a rainy day."

"Here it is, right at our doorstep, and you haven't shown the slightest interest…"

Almost immediately she apologized.

"I'm sorry, dear. I *didn't* sleep very well last night. How selfish you must think me. Of course you're right, we'll spend hours and hours at the Louvre when it's less clement weather. Oh, I *am* a bossy woman!"

"You are not. You're a love. I'm sorry you had a bad night."

"Not a bad night…just not a very good one. All right, this morning we'll visit the Eiffel Tower and all the surrounding area. As you say, it's a fine day, and we must take advantage of the sun so long as it's considerate enough to shine for us."

"And maybe this afternoon we can go to the old Marais district, to the Place de Vosges, where I understand Victor Hugo's house is? Plus, naturally I'd like to have a look at the Place de la Bastille."

Her aunt laughed. "Some of those spots are rather far afield of each other."

"Yes, I realize that."

"Don't worry. Paris is full of taxis."

"Can't we take the Metro?"

"Sorry about that," Louisa said dryly, "but I'm not any fonder of the Paris subway system than I am of New York's. You won't get me on the Metro."

"We can walk a good deal of the way, though, can't we?"

"Don't you worry, we'll be doing enough walking. There's a cab stand just off the Concorde. We'll get one there to take us to the Champs de Mars."

When they went downstairs Iris took her letters and postcards to the desk. *"Bonjour,* Pierre," she said to the concierge.

"Bonjour, Mademoiselle. *Comment Ça va aujourd'hui?"*

"Merci, très bien. Je passe un bon moment."

He smiled appreciatively, and his glance went beyond her to Louisa, who was waiting on a small chaise.

"Bonjour, Madame. Your niece speaks our language very well."

He stamped the letters and the postcards, told Iris the amount of the postage, and wished them a pleasant day.

"You do manage the language beautifully," Louisa said admiringly, as they walked down the Rue Castiglione.

"Only passably, shame on me. Mostly, I say everything in the present tense. If I lived here, though, I'd pick it up quickly."

"Would you like to live here?"

"Yes," Iris said promptly. "Oh, I know I'm seeing only the bright side of the coin. Visitors always do. They don't notice the *clochards,* the winos, the hookers, or the interiors of some of the buildings that look so gorgeous and picturesque from the street, but which are probably rotting inside."

They had come to the Rue de Rivoli.

"Look at this sumptuousness," Iris said, gesturing toward the glittering shops on the arcaded avenue with the intaglioed stone that served as pavement. "This is what we see, or else the quaintness in the old, old sections. We sigh and are ecstatic…but it's only the facade."

"Well, you do seem to have your feet on the ground," her aunt observed. "That's very astute. You mean, of course, that you're able to be realistic about it."

"Sure." She grinned. "Just the same, though, I'd like to live here. I imagine I could take the bad with the good."

"So pretty and with a mind too," her aunt said, returning the grin. "Will wonders never cease?"

"Oh, I'm a marvel. But why not, with such genes? An aunt like you?" She pointed. "Is that the cab stand down there?"

"Yes. Only there's no cab. We'll have to wait."

It wasn't for very long. A taxi, disgorging a natty passenger with a pencil-thin mustache and an attache case, accommodated them after only a few minutes had passed.

"The Champs de Mars, please," Louisa said, and the driver shot forward before they even had a chance to settle in their seats.

"Will we see Napoleon's tomb?" Iris asked, as they circled the Concorde. "That's near where we're going, isn't it?"

The cab driver peered in his rear view mirror. "You want to see Les Invalides?" he demanded, craning his neck for abrief look at her.

"According to my map, it's—"

"I take you there," he said heartily. "Everyone has to see Napoleon's tomb."

And from then on he didn't stop talking, somewhat disjointedly, in atrociously-accented English, and in a loud, booming voice.

"American," he stated, rather than asked.

"Yes. *Oui.*"

"Late for Americans. And for Les Anglais. They come in summer, *les étrangères.*"

"I suppose so," Louisa agreed.

"What?" he shouted.

"I said they…I said yes, I suppose so."

"I don't mind. Good for business."

He made a sharp left turn, at which Iris found herself practically in her aunt's lap.

"How long you have been here?" the driver asked with ear-splitting cordiality.

"Three days," Iris informed him.

"What?" he shouted again.

"Three days. *Trois jours.*"

He laughed almost affectionately. *"Trois jours…*then you have not seen *anything!*"

"Yes, we have," Iris yelled accommodatingly. The poor man's hearing was probably permanently impaired due to the horrendous din of Paris traffic.

He was good-naturedly scornful. "What have you seen in three days?"

"Uh…well, Notre Dame, and the Ile St. Louis, and St. Germain, and…"

He shrugged grudgingly. *"Eh bien…*it's a start."

They were crossing the river.

"Soon now, Les Invalides," he instructed them in stentorian tones.

And then, slowing up, he drove them past the barracks-like expanse of what had once been the hospital that housed the sick and mutilated of Louis XIV's men of arms and where blood-soaked bandages had piled up in the courtyards.

"Les Invalides," their obliging driver cried out, and thrust an arm out of his window with a flourish.

"Ah yes," Iris said, at the top of her lungs, while her aunt concealed a mirthful smile.

Then, "Le Tombeau de Napoleon," he announced dramatically. He shook his head admiringly. *"Regardez Ça…"*

He gestured toward the high, domed monument, with its soaring spire, as if he were presenting them with it as a personal gift.

He brought the vehicle to a grinding, shuddering halt. And before Iris could object that, at the moment, they had just wanted to have a look at Napoleon's tomb on their way to the Champs de Mars, he shut off his meter and turned to them with a beaming face.

"Beautiful inside," he informed them. "There lies Bonaparte, and his son, l'Aiglon." He became quite emotional. "You know what Napoleon inscribed in his *testament?* No? He said, 'I wish my body to be laid to rest on the banks of the Seine, among the French people I love so well…'"

He sighed. "And there he is to this day." He glanced at his meter. "That will be twelve francs, Madame."

"But we wanted to—"

Louisa interrupted what Iris had started to say.

"Thank you," she said, paying the driver.

"Thank *you,*" he replied, pocketing the fare and what had doubtless been a handsome tip. With an expansive smile that revealed two gleaming gold teeth, he ground gears with a resounding snarl and went roaring away into the distance.

"Well, that was a short ride," Louisa said, tittering.

"I'm sorry," Iris apologized. "I didn't mean to take matters into my own hands."

"It's all right," her aunt said, overcome with amusement. "He was just so *funny.* Most of them are inclined to be surly, but this one simply killed us with kindness."

She wiped mirthful tears from her eyes. "To hear you shrieking at him like that…I thought I'd die."

How nice, Iris thought. Her aunt was up again, where earlier she had been down…how nice to see her giggling like this.

"Now that we're here shall we go inside?"

"Of course," Louisa agreed. "We're on our way to where we wanted to go anyway."

The interior of the tomb, with its lofty, vaulted rotunda, its niches and crypts and imperial banners, was almost deserted. Only a handful of sightseers circled the sunken recess in which Bonaparte and his twenty-year-old son, the Duke of Reichstad, lay side by side.

Iris gazed down at the red granite sarcophagus wherein reposed the earthly remains of the Little Corporal, and recalled what he had said in one of his last hours.

"Our hour is marked, and no one can claim a moment of life beyond what fate has predestined."

It could have been his epitaph, she thought, and shivered. It could be everyone's epitaph.

Outside again, she was glad to see the sun, and the trees with their leaves whispering and leave the great, and the dead, to their eternal solitude.

"Somber and solemn," Louisa commented. "Well, now we've done our duty by our friendly neighborhood cab driver, let's cut over to the Avenue la Bourdonnais and we'll be at the Champs de Mars."

And so they were, only moments later, walking amidst its trim lawns and sculptured shrubbery, with the great iron pyramid of the Eiffel Tower piercing the sky. It was so familiar, and yet such a shock to be really seeing it for the first time. Every girder like the rib of a dinosaur, it was monstrous…and yet tremendously impressive.

Between the four gigantic feet at its base was a magnificent view of the Palais de Chaillot across the river, shimmering in the sunlight like a mirage.

"Well?" Louisa asked, looking up at the tower.

"It's crazy. But it wouldn't be Paris without it."

"No it wouldn't. Shall I buy you a balloon?" she asked, indicating some of the garish stands where souvenirs were for sale

"No, but I'd like an ice."

"So would I," Louisa said, and they went over to a stall that dealt in such things.

"Strawberry for me," Iris decided, and her aunt chose lemon. They sat down on a bench and, with relish, ate their glacés.

There were litter baskets at regular intervals, but it was clear that here, as in New York, they were largely ignored. The pavement was strewn with discarded rubbish.

"Too bad," Louisa commented. "Really, people can be so unthinking." She kicked a soft drink can out of her path. "All right, let's cross over to the Trocadero side."

When they had done so the vista, with the Eiffel Tower on one side of the Seine and the Palais de Chaillot, on its lofty rise, opposite it on the other side, was a study in contrast.

Here, there was a stately formality, with the glimmer of bright blue water in a rectangular sunken pool, graveled walks bordered with flowery lanes of plantings, with the two widely-spaced wings of the Palais, pristinely white, dominating the overall picture.

When they had walked the long distance up to the 20th century Palais—where more recent history had been made—the view was breathtaking.

"Let's just sit for a while," Louisa suggested.

"Let's sit for a year or so," Iris murmured.

"You'll want to go in the Musée de l'Homme," her aunt told her. "I find it fascinating and so will you."

"What else is in the Palais?"

"Oh, all sorts of things. Fashion shows are sometimes held here. But there's a museum of arts and traditions you'd probably be interested in. We can do both places."

They only "did" the Musée de l'Homme, which was, as Louisa had declared, fascinating indeed. But after that Iris was not to be pried from the great stone terrace between the two wings of the Palais, and they spent another half hour there.

It was the view, of course. It was the height at which the Palais de Chaillot stood, opening up a sweeping panorama of the city.

Finally Louisa insisted that they really must tear themselves away. "It's after one, and there are other things on our schedule."

"Yes, you're right."

"And now the Place de Vosges?"

"All right with you?"

"Fine with me. You want to see Victor Hugo's house? You shall see his house. Anyway, it's a wondrous place, a great, noble square of quintessential beauty. I seem to recall that you also expressed a desire to go to the Place de la Bastille."

"If we can work it in."

"We can, and will. Somewhere in between we'll find a cafe and have a bit of lunch. Nothing much…a *croque monsieur* and a cold drink. Let's get ourselves up to the avenue and find a cab. What a lovely day! I assure you, it can rain in this city for days on end, and generally when you've planned only a few days to stay."

"Fortune favors us," Iris said gaily, and so it seemed to, for they found a cruising taxi the moment they got to the Avenue President Wilson. Its driver was one of the surly ones, but who cared?

At least I don't have to scream myself hoarse, Iris thought, and reminded herself that tomorrow she would have to buy some more rolls of film for her camera.

Eight

At the end of another long, wearying but rewarding day, and at just short of seven o'clock, Louisa said, "Let's not bother going back to the hotel. We'll find a place for dinner somewhere around here."

"Suits me," Iris said gratefully. "I don't particularly cotton to the idea of changing clothes and fixing my dumb face. Frankly, I'm pooped."

"Is it catching up with you?"

"You mean the accumulation of three days of rubbernecking and walking blisters on my feet? Not in any way I mind. Heaven forbid. It's mostly the way your mind gets filled with impressions until you feel you'll explode."

"Iris, it seems to me I recall a restaurant in this vicinity. We could have dinner there if I can find it."

They were at the Place de la Bastille where, of course, there had been no Bastille for almost two hundred years and where now there stood, in a drab and undramatic spot, an unremarkable column to mark the infamous prison a maddened populace had once stormed.

"I think," Louisa said, "that the restaurant I have in mind was on the Rue St. Antoine."

"Let's have a look around," Iris suggested, and after walking some distance her aunt said yes, this looked familiar.

"That little church up ahead…I'm sure this is about where it was. Of course it may no longer be there…though in Paris everything generally is always there, year after year."

A minute later she cried, "That's it!"

A sign on a royal-blue canopy read L'AUBERGE BRETAGNE.

"That means fish," Louisa said, delighted. "Yes, I remember we had a very good meal here."

"It looks neighborhood French."

"It should be. This isn't tourist territory."

Inside, their greeting was cordial: A rotund and genial *patron* led them to a small banquette by a window where, in the gathering dusk, they were able to look out at the fine old trees that bordered the street.

There were fresh flowers on their table, exposed beams overhead, and a fieldstone hearth at the farther end of the room. A convivial waiter brought over two gloriously chilled martinis, slipped their menus unobtrusively to one side of the table, and left them to enjoy their drinks, over which they discussed the events of the day.

"What did you like best?" Louisa asked, and when Iris said the Place de Vosges, she nodded. "It's an architectural gem," she agreed. "You saw Victor Hugo's house and that of Madame de Sévigné. The whole area is steeped in history, some of it very bloody—the head of Madame de Lamballe on a pike, for example, and the tumbrils rumbling over the cobblestones to the Temple."

She gave her niece a slightly defensive glance. "When I married Henry," she said, "I was a little ignoramus. I knew so *little*. Henry, though, was a scholar. He was the only teacher I ever learned anything from. He made me a total person."

She finished her drink, said, "I just felt I wanted you to know that, Iris," and opened her *carte*.

"Shall we order?" she suggested. "Or do you want another drink?"

"No, let's order. I'm starved."

"Then I shall have the écrévisses a la nage."

"Which is what?"

"Crayfish. They're delicious."

"Forgive me, but yuk."

"Order it for me if he comes over, will you? I'm going to find the washroom. I'll start with the moules marinière."

She disappeared into nether regions and Iris studied the menu. She had a passion for soft-shelled crabs and they were listed, but were they in season?

The waiter, seeing her upturned look, rushed over solicitously.

"You wish to order, Mademoiselle?"

"Are the soft-shelled crabs in season?"

"*Mais oui* certainly, Mademoiselle."

"Then I'll have that. And for an appetizer, some steamers."

He was busy scribbling on a pad.

"My aunt will have moules marinière to start. And then the… écrévisses a la…"

"A la nage," he finished for her.

He bowed, like the son of the son of the son of one of Napoleon's servicemen, and then left her alone with a memory of his brilliant, Gallic smile.

It brought to mind the title of one of Francoise Sagan's novels, *A Certain Smile,* and unbidden, unexpected and certainly unwanted, there flashed in Iris's mind another smile…that of Paul Chandon. The quick vision of those upturned lips, those flashing white teeth in a tanned face was so vivid that she closed her eyes against it. When she opened them again her aunt was sliding into her seat.

"You ordered?" she asked.

"Yes. I'm having steamers and soft-shelled crabs."

•••

When they were once again back at the Place Vendôme, the beautiful square was flood-lit and as entrancing as a scene from a Pisarro watercolor. The obelisk at its center, rising high and ever impressive, seemed to be trying to touch the stars.

There was a soft, cooling breeze, and the timeless smell of old stone. It was a night for exploring, for adventure. It was not a night in which to go, long before the witching hour, indoors and, tamely, to bed.

"Coming?" Louisa called.

"Right with you."

Iris followed her aunt into the hotel, but turned to give a last look at the bewitching radiance outside…and at the soft Paris sky, with a crescent moon whitely shining.

What would it be like to be in Paris and at the same time to be in love? On a night like this, to venture forth, arm in arm with one's beloved…and forget about minutes, hours…days, even?

At the desk the night concierge reached in their box and handed them their mail. "Yes, and some telephone messages," he said.

Iris had two letters, one from her parents and one from Jeff.

"Letters from the home front," she told her aunt, but Louisa was busy scanning the phone messages the concierge had given her.

"What did you get?" she asked her aunt, and Louisa looked up.

"Oh, *that's* nice," she said happily. "There are two messages from Paul Chandon. He's phoned twice, it appears. At four this afternoon and again only an hour ago."

"Great," Iris said unenthusiastically, and as they rode upstairs in the ornate little lift, she studied her aunt's face, remarking the rise in color to her cheeks, and the small, almost furtive smile that rested on her lips.

When they reached their quarters, Louisa turned the key in the lock. The salon was in darkness and she turned on the overhead light. Then, switching on several lamps, turned it off again.

"I think we could do with a nightcap," she said gaily. "Let's visit for a bit before going to bed—post mortems about our day."

"All right."

Louisa sank down on the sofa. She kicked off her shoes and opened the bottle of Courvoisier, filling the two glasses. "We had a very good day, didn't we?"

"We always do when we're together."

"Sit down, dear, we'll have our little nip and then turn in."

Iris sat down obediently.

"What did you like best today?" Louisa asked brightly.

We've already gone through all that, Iris thought, but refrained from saying so.

"Everything," she said instead. "It was all perfect."

"You liked the Place de Vosges, I could tell that. It's one of my favorite spots in the world. My first love—and you can quote me on this, Iris—is the Piazza san Marco in Venice. I'll take you there some day."

If, Iris thought somberly, some young man with ulterior motives doesn't snap you up with a view toward feathering his own nest. Someone like Paul Chandon.

Later, in her room, she read her two letters and then lay, trying to sleep, watching the moonlit shimmer that came through the tall, handsome windows.

Tomorrow morning, without any doubt, Paul Chandon would follow up on his two telephone calls of today and it would begin all over again.

And Jeff was worried about me in Paris, she thought, stifling a compulsion to laugh hysterically. He hadn't said so, but she knew he had been thinking about Parisian men following her about on the street.

Who would have thought it would be Aunt Louisa who would capitulate to a pair of dark eyes and a dazzling smile? Who in the world could have suspected that her aunt would languish, like a Victorian heroine, over someone young enough to be her son?

Don't think, she told herself.

The way her aunt's eyes had lighted up when she got those messages...

Don't think. Just go to sleep.

I never bargained for anything like this, Iris told herself, tossing. It was ridiculous. It was grotesque.

I *said,* don't *think,* she told herself viciously, and pulled the covers over her head.

Nine

Halfway through breakfast the next morning, the telephone shrilled in Louisa's room and she got up so quickly that she almost upset her coffee cup.

"Excuse me while I take that," she said hastily, and rushed into her bedroom, her peignoir swishing along the carpet.

Then her door slammed shut.

The call was, dollars to doughnuts, from Paul Chandon, Iris thought grimly.

I feel like crying, she thought. Or tearing my hair out, strand by strand.

She never would have imagined, in her wildest dreams, that her Aunt Louisa could so easily forget twenty-two years of a happy marriage…and fall, like a ripe plum, into the wily arms of a…

Of a Parisian stud.

Bleakly, she noted the passing minutes on her watch, and after ten of them had ticked by, got up and paced the floor.

What was she saying to him? What was *he* saying?

There was a sudden vision of Paul Chandon, of his tall stature, his easy and assured posture, his dark eyes and his flashing smile.

She tried to picture herself, widowed and melancholy, and then meeting someone like Paul Chandon. What would be her own reaction?

How could you imagine yourself forty-six years old and widowed, she thought impatiently. It was impossible. She couldn't even envision the day after tomorrow, much less twenty-two years from now.

Yet reluctantly, after much reflection, she had to admit that, under her aunt's circumstances, she might regard Paul Chandon acquisitively.

But I wouldn't trust an utter stranger, not under *any* circumstances, she told herself passionately. Someone you met in a cafe…someone you knew nothing *about*.

Her aunt's door opened, so she sat down quickly.

"I'll just get rid of this cold coffee and have some fresh," Louisa said cheerily. "Do you suppose I'd be arrested if I threw it out the window?"

"I wouldn't chance it. Pour it down the john."

"I don't suppose it will hurt this plant," Louisa said merrily, and dumped the gelid liquid into a potted plant on the window sill.

Then she sat down again, poured herself some coffee from the steaming silver urn and announced that Paul Chandon had just called.

"He apologized profusely for having to cancel our plans for last night," she explained. "And he would like us to have lunch with him at one-thirty today. That sounds nice, doesn't it?"

"At the same time," Iris pointed out coolly, "it will break our day very neatly in half. Where are we supposed to lunch with him?"

"At a place on the Rue de Lille. *La Chandelle*. I know it only by hearsay, but it's a favorite of Left Bank writers and editors. It has an éclat, like the Brasserie Lipp."

"Did he ask for both of us to go?" Iris asked slowly.

Louisa looked astonished…but then again, Iris thought, as if she might be faking surprise. "What do you mean, both of us?" she demanded.

"I just wondered."

"What's wrong with you? Of course he wants both of us." She gave her niece a searching look. "Are you still worrying about the fact that we weren't introduced properly to him?" she asked, narrowing her eyes. "Is that what's—"

Iris pleated her breakfast napkin with nervous fingers. "I'm not sold on men who…"

"Who what?" her aunt demanded. "Men who what?"

"Oh, never *mind.*"

There was a little silence. Then, "I like him," Louisa said quietly. "Can't you let it go at that?"

"If you say so."

"No. Not if I say so." She gestured. "I'm sorry. I should have consulted you before I accepted. I just didn't think there would be any reason why you wouldn't want to have a civilized lunch in a civilized restaurant with a civilized man."

"No reason," Iris said quickly. She was now sorry she had made an issue of it. She certainly didn't want her aunt to go off without her to spend some time with that designing man.

"No reason at all," she repeated. "Where is this Rue de Lille?"

"Not far from where we were the other day," her aunt said. "The day we went to Notre Dame."

And the day we met Paul Chandon, Iris thought resentfully. The day everything changed, and my worries began.

"Super," she said, summoning a smile to her face. "In that case, why don't we walk up the Right Bank this time and cross over at the Pont d'Arcole? If we do that we can see the flower markets. I'd like to."

"Oh, you've been studying your map," her aunt cried. "Good girl. Before I know it, you'll be showing *me* about Paris."

"I doubt it. But yes, I'm getting there, and I'm almost sure that, if I had to, I could get about quite easily."

"Needless to say, I'm pleased. And now we must get dressed and ready to leave."

They did so at just before ten, and today, sadly, the sun was hiding behind fast-moving clouds in a slatey sky.

"It looks like rain," Iris said. "Oh dear. Shall I go back and get an umbrella?"

"Yes, do. Mine's on top of my suitcase. A folding one."

When she came down again, with both umbrellas, there were indeed a few drops of rain.

"I'll have a fit if our luck changes," Iris said disappointedly. "What do you think?"

"After all, it's nearing the middle of September. It could very well change for the worse. I hope not."

But by the time they had reached the Rue de Rivoli, the rain had stopped. Iris crossed her fingers. And as a matter of fact, the sky, ominous and mushrooming with those great, vaporous clouds, was still beautiful, wildly wonderful and, in a way, even more spectacular.

Yet, no matter how you looked at it, autumn was on its way. It gave Iris a stab of melancholy. If autumn came, was winter far behind? When this city was cold and snowy, and all the trees sere and leafless, she wouldn't be here. She would have been long gone.

"No," she murmured, not even knowing she was saying it aloud.

"What's that?" her aunt asked.

"I was just thinking about a time when I wouldn't be here any more."

"That's the way I wanted you to feel. And I hope that—"

"That what?"

"Um…oh, high hopes, high hopes. Shall we walk through the Tuileries? We have loads of time. We can go as far as the Carrousel and then make our way back for a look at one of my pet haunts, the Palais-Royal. Afterwards we'll wander all the way down the Right Bank."

The Tuileries gardens, where once princesses and dauphins had strolled, was a lovely park, with its riotous gardens, turquoise pools, burbling fountains and flowery scents. The Carrousel, a miniscule version of the Arc de Triomphe, was a small delight.

"A pretty place," Louisa said reflectively. "I've often sat here with a book, or the morning newspaper, while Henry smoked his endless cigars. Okay, let's go over to the Palais-Royal. You will adore it. I've often thought about taking an apartment there, a pièd a terre. Henry and I did some talking about it, but never more than that."

"Colette lived there," Iris said. "And Cocteau too."

"A lot of prestigious people lived, and live there. I can imagine the rents."

"Where does Paul Chandon live?" Iris asked suddenly. The thought had just occurred to her. She was really more or less thinking aloud, and was very much startled when her aunt answered, right away and very casually, "Somewhere in the Rue Jacob." And then added, "It's a place many young people like to quarter themselves."

So she even knows where he lives, Iris thought, stunned. She even knew that…

The two of them had certainly covered a lot of ground in a single meeting.

She followed her aunt, darkly speculating, and was only roused from her tumult of thoughts by the sight of a gilded statue of Joan of Arc at a crossing on the Rue de Rivoli. Brightly gleaming, even in this overcast day, the golden Maid, on a golden steed, burst upon her eyes like a fanciful dream.

"You haven't seen it before because we haven't walked in this direction," Louisa said, smiling at Iris's excitement as she got out her camera. "It's a nice little surprise, isn't it?"

"I just love it!"

"And now we'll go up this street to the Rue St. Honoré to see the house that Richelieu built. Come along."

A few blocks later the Palais-Royal presented itself in all its splendid perfection. Beyond its golden portals lay a colonnaded courtyard of stupendous beauty, in back of which rose the tall-pillared, gilded palace of the eminent cardinal.

The whole vista of the long, large rectangle, sequestered as it was by its columned promenades, gave it the appearance of a hidden island, complete unto itself in all the hurly-burly of Paris.

"Like a secret garden," Iris said ecstatically. "Can we go inside the courtyard?"

"Um hum. Come, we'll amble along one of the loggias."

Louisa consulted her watch. "It's eleven-thirty. That gives us two hours before meeting Paul. Enough time, granted, but you'll want to spend some time at the flower market along the quays—that is, if it's not a bird market today. So we mustn't linger too long."

•••

La Chandelle, on the Rue de Lille, was a good bit more impressive than the place Paul Chandon had chosen on the Ile St. Louis. It looked expensive, smelled expensive, and had a decided aura of sophistication.

The maitre d' asked, with suave cordiality, if they were expecting someone.

"Monsieur Chandon's table," Louisa answered. "Has he arrived yet?"

"Please," the man said pleasantly. "This way, Mesdames."

He led them past a polished bar and through to a bright, cheerful room with great bowls of silvery, dried flowers massed in stunning profusion. There was sparkling napery on the tables, the gleam of crystal and silver and a general air of easy affluence.

In spite of this, Iris noted that several of the men diners were in casual attire, with carelessly-worn jackets and ties loosened. At least two men wore no ties at all.

You wouldn't see that in Manhattan, she thought, where a great emphasis was placed on neckties. Women might go half naked, but the strictures for men were merciless enforced.

She rather approved of the more relaxed status quo here, and then saw Paul Chandon, standing at their approach. He himself was without a tie, though he had on a lightweight jacket that was unbuttoned.

Two days had passed since she had seen him, thought it seemed, for some reason, far more than that. She gave him a quick, critical look and, whatever she might think of him, had to acknowledge that this Paul Chandon was a strikingly handsome man. Coming to terms with that fact, she accepted it, and promised herself that she would be very understanding with her aunt. Lesser women than Louisa had capitulated to men not as prepossessing in their appearance.

And I will be nice, she told herself. I will be charming, agreeable, and utterly adorable.

A mischievous thought came to her. How about going all out and being *so* utterly adorable that Paul Chandon would find her too enchanting to resist?

In short, seduce the would-be lover of her own aunt.

Now *that* sounds too much like a Feydeau farce, she decided with an inward grin, and answered Paul's greeting.

"Hello yourself," she said gaily. "And how are you, Monsieur Chandon?"

He was very well, he said, standing like a sentinel until the women were seated. "But I am sorry about last night. Something came up that was totally unexpected. So I thought that, at least, I could make up for it just a little bit by this."

He added, hastily, "I mean, naturally, make it up to myself for the loss of your charming company last evening."

"Don't give it another thought," Louisa said. "We had a very pleasant day and had dinner at a restaurant I remembered from previous trips."

She outlined their itinerary of yesterday, and when she mentioned the *Auberge Bretagne* Paul's face lit up.

"But I know it," he said. "I have been there several times."

"Marvelous crayfish," Louisa commented. She looked about. "I can imagine that there will be *enormous* portions in this pretty, hospitable place and I am counting calories."

"Count them when you return to New York," he replied, smiling.

She laughed, and turned to Iris. "Shall we have our bread and cheese in our rooms tonight?" she suggested.

"I'm all for it. And afterwards I'll wash my hair. It's way past due. I'm letting myself go in the most awful way. Paris has laid a spell on me."

"I was almost sure it would," Paul said.

"Oh, were you?"

He laughed, didn't pursue the subject, and told the waiter who came over that the ladies would have very dry martinis and he himself would have a bock.

Iris was dying of curiosity to know what "a bock" was, but she would sooner have cut her tongue out than ask. And when their drinks came, Paul's bock turned out to be beer.

So now I know what a bock is, she thought, and decided that her knowledge of the world was improving.

"I suppose you have bought some Paris dresses," Paul said to Iris as they sipped their drinks.

"Not a one. Nor will I. Oh, a scarf or two, probably. But in the main, presents to take back home."

"You have many friends?"

"Yes, I guess I do, friends and acquaintances. We all do, don't we?"

"We do when we're young," he said.

"Why not when we're older?"

"Because when we are older, circumstances change."

She gave him a curious glance. He was certainly paying a bit more attention to her today. For what reason?

She narrowed her eyes. To get on the good side of her? And would he next produce some friend of his, saying, "I thought it would be nice if there were four of us."

"Friends," Paul continued, "loom rather large in our scheme of things. But I know people, of all ages, who have joined the Peace Corps and left friends, and family, behind. Friends don't make a life, Mademoiselle."

"They help," Louisa said ruminatively. "But they can't make up for the most important things."

Like the loss of a loved one, Iris thought. No one could make up for something like that.

"You have not been to the Beaubourg?" Paul asked, with a small smile.

"Not yet, but it's on the agenda," Louisa replied. "What do you think of it, Paul?"

"What do I think of it? That it's terrible, ugly and garish…and yet exactly what Paris needed."

He laughed. "You will have to make up your own minds, when you go there. Naturally I miss the proximity of Les Halles, which is now in Rungis."

"I'll miss it too," Louisa said. "How many times have I gone there, after a long night's wandering. I can't believe it's gone."

Then Louisa and Paul compared notes about all the good times each had had at the former Paris central market, and all the good times they had had at other places.

Meanwhile Louisa, Iris noted, sparkled, grew rosy and animated and said, yes, she would have another martini, thank you.

"Mademoiselle?"

"One's my limit during the day, thank you."

The second drink for the other two arrived, and the conversation between Louisa and Paul resumed. But there was something else

Iris was aware of. Every time she looked up from sipping the single martini she was nursing, she was sure that Paul Chandon's eyes had been on her, and that when she looked in his direction, they slid away quickly.

Now what was he up to, she wondered uncomfortably, and was vastly relieved when it was decided that they would give the order for their lunch.

Iris studied the gigantic menu and said she would have paté de maison and steak tartare.

"With all these goodies?" Louisa cried. "You must be coming down with something!"

"It's all I want."

"It can happen that someone in love loses the appetite," Paul hazarded. "That could be the answer."

"Not for me," Iris said tartly.

"Too bad," he said, with one of his teasing smiles. "I am sorry to hear that, Mademoiselle."

"I wouldn't want you to lose sleep over it," she answered evenly.

"I will try not to."

He threw down his carte. "I have made my selection."

Louisa, raising contrite green eyes, said that she was still wavering. "Forgive me, but I'm having rather a struggle."

"There is no hurry," Paul said gently. "In fact, quite the opposite."

"But I must make up my mind," she said, avidly scanning her menu, and after a minute or two made her decision, laughing at her greed.

Paul gave the order to the starched waiter and, in doing so, was very much the assured host.

"*Et pour moi,*" he finished, "asparagus vinaigrette. *Après Ça,* filets de poisson poches au vin blanc."

"*Très bien, Monsieur. Et maintenant, le vin?*"

"*Pour Madame et moi-même,* une carafe de Chenin Blanc."

The waiter scribbled.

"Pour Mademoiselle, une demi-bouteille de Bordeaux rouge."

"Merci, Monsieur."

After that, Paul leaned back, puffing on his Gauloise. "Have you done any sightseeing today?" he asked.

"Yes, of course," Louisa said. "Among other things, I introduced Iris to the Palais-Royal."

"Ah, the Palais-Royal. It's a gem."

He tapped ashes in a small porcelain tray that bore the house name. "It's interesting how the centuries come and go, but change, in some aspects, so little. Today, more than three centuries after that palace was built, the general outlines of it are still intact. Did you know that the eminent cardinal suffered from disabling headaches?"

"I seem to have heard that he also suffered from terrible hemorrhoids," Iris said bluntly.

"True," Paul said, with one of his dazzling smiles. "Only, since we are at lunch, I had not meant to bring that up."

"Leave it to Iris to call a spade a spade," Louisa said. "It's all right, dear, we all know that about poor Richelieu."

"I imagine most of us know of his outrageous extravagance," Paul commented.. "His household—servants and aides— numbered something like twelve hundred persons. That, by anyone's standards, is living in style."

"While the poor went without bread," Iris observed.

"While the poor went without bread," he agreed. "But they finally decided that they would have their bread and they took their revenge. The Revolution and the guillotine."

He smiled. "When I was young, just a young boy, I read a book that remains to this day one of my favorites of all literature."

"What was that, Paul?" Louisa asked.

"It began," he said, "with these lines: 'It was the best of times, it was the worst of times, it was the age of foolishness, it was the epoch of belief, it was the epoch of incredulity, it was the season of Light, it was the season of Darkness, it was the spring of hope, it was the winter of despair…'"

"A Tale of Two Cities," Iris said, and wished he hadn't quoted that. It was too near to her, too dear to her and to have Paul Chandon, for whom she had little regard, recite those almost sacred lines—and further, to know them so well—endowed him with a sensitivity she was disinclined to acknowledge.

"Yes, of course," he said, and gave her another one of his maddeningly teasing smiles. "You not only speak French very well but you are also very proficient in literature. Victor Hugo… Dickens…"

But before Iris could think of a suitable retort, the waiter wheeled over a cart and, with grandiose flourishes, began serving their meal.

A meal which was very good indeed 'by anyone's standards,' Iris thought, paraphrasing Paul's earlier phrase.

Paul himself, however, seemed appetite-less, and ate only sparingly, leaving most of the food on his plate.

At something like 100 francs per portion, this seemed a rather cavalier attitude to Iris. Also, his behavior, so insouciant on the day they had met him, had subtly changed. He was not abstracted… it wasn't that. He talked in lively fashion, but he seemed, at odd moments, thoughtful and…careful, Iris decided.

As if every move of his counted. As if he must do everything exactly right, without mistake…and so was not totally relaxed.

When they were having their coffee and the brandies Paul ordered with it, he said, "And now may we discuss our postponed dinner together? I am so sorry it had to be delayed, and I hope you will forgive me. But unless for some reason it is out of the question for you, may we have dinner tomorrow evening?" He gave a wry little smile. "And this time, nothing will intervene…at least on my part."

"That would be lovely, Paul."

He looked at Iris. "Mademoiselle?"

"Why not?"

Why not indeed? There were many reasons why not, but she was powerless to voice them. It seemed she was stuck with Paul Chandon, whether she liked it or not, unless she wanted to bow out and leave her aunt to the mercies of this upstart.

"Wonderful," he said warmly. "If you have no objections, I thought it would be pleasant to dine on the Butte. The Place du Tertre."

"It would be perfect," Louisa said enthusiastically. "Of course it's not the best of weather today. If it rains tomorrow the Place du Tertre wouldn't do, would it?"

"It won't rain tomorrow," he promised. "It will rain late tonight, but tomorrow will be fair again."

"How do you know that?" Iris asked.

"I have listened to the weather reports on and off."

"Where I come from, the weather reports are generally unreliable."

"They are generally unreliable here too, but this time I am inclined to believe them."

His flashing smile came once more.

"Because I want them to be correct," he added.

"I hope you're right," Louisa said. "There's nothing I'd like more than an evening on the Butte, and Iris will adore it."

When they finally rose to go, Iris's watch showed her that it was now after three. Most of the afternoon gone, she thought discontentedly.

And her aunt, being ushered out by a gallant Paul, was undeniably more impressed with him than ever.

It certainly looked like a losing battle.

Outside on the street, Louisa said, after thanking Paul for a "lovely, lovely lunch," that if they were going to Montmartre and the Butte tomorrow, it would be a good idea to start early.

"Do you think you could possibly manage to call at the hotel at around five? So that Iris can see the transformation of the city as night falls. It's really part of the whole thing."

"I will be there at five on the dot."

He looked down at them. "What are you going to do now?" he asked.

"Oh…I did think I might hop over to the Quai des Grand Augustins, since we're so near it," Louisa said. "I saw something in one of the antique shops and I'd like to look at it again."

"Well then," he said, "would I be in the way if I went along with you? And then I will take a taxi back to where I have a four-thirty appointment."

"Come along," Louisa said, looking pleased. "Maybe you can help me make up my mind."

And all like that, Iris thought, trying to resign herself. So much for the rest of the day: By the time Paul Chandon left them it would be late afternoon.

The whole day shot to blazes.

Not that she minded walking along the Left Bank quays again. The river was like a narcotic for her. It was something she would never tire of.

It was just that she had done her duty, been affable at lunch, smiled until it hurt, and they still weren't free of Paul Chandon.

I do not like feeling like a fifth wheel, she told herself. And it was exactly what she felt like. Excess baggage. Paul Chandon's smiles were not for her…they were for her aunt.

As if he sensed Iris's resentment, today he chose to walk between them, so that she had to carry on a conversation with him whether she liked it or not.

"What was it you saw in that shop in the Grands Augustins?" he was asking Louisa.

"A clock that seemed to me to be something of a find," she said. "Circa 1700. Wonderful marquetry. Hideously expensive, but I did rather fall in love with it."

"Did you like it?" Paul asked Iris.

"I know nothing about antiques," she said.

"I should think you would know a great deal since your aunt is so knowledgeable about them."

"Do you know about them?" she asked indifferently.

"A little something."

Bully for you, Iris thought.

"You are wearing your hair differently today," he commented.

"Am I?"

"Yes, the part is on the other side."

"Imagine you being so observant," Louisa said, laughing delightedly. "Men are generally so unnoticing."

"Women only think they are," Paul said, smiling. "For example, Madame, when you came into the restaurant earlier today you were wearing earrings. And now you are not."

"I'm not because they began to hurt so I took them off. Well, you certainly keep your eyes open, Paul."

She pointed. "There's a Bateau Mouche," she said, looking toward the river. "Not very many people on it today."

"There will be more in the evening, for dinner and dancing," he assured her.

"I suppose so. I haven't been on one in years."

"Neither have I," he admitted, and turned to Iris. "Have you indulged in that little pleasure yet, Mademoiselle?"

"Not yet."

"I suppose you will, sooner or later."

"I suppose so."

He smiled teasingly. "It should be with someone you are in love with," he told her. "At night, when the city is lit up like a shower of stars."

"Really?"

"Yes, it's one of the things lovers do here. But since you assured me that you were not in love with anyone, perhaps you won't bother with the Bateau Mouche."

And before she could answer him, he turned again to her aunt. "And here we are at the antique shops," he said. "Which one has your expensive treasure, Madame?"

"Just up ahead."

"I hope your clock is still there."

"I hope it's not. If it is, I'll be tempted to buy it."

But when they went into the shop the clock was still there, and Louisa, after circling around it, asked Paul's opinion.

"Yes," he said, after an inspection of it. "It's a very good piece."

"Shall I succumb?" Louisa asked him.

He asked the owner its price, and when told, whistled softly.

"It's a lot of money," he said to Louisa.

"Yes, but it's not overpriced."

"No, it's not overpriced. But the Customs…"

"Yes," Louisa sighed. "The Customs."

She thought a minute and then said briskly, "But I shall have it." She conferred with the owner of the shop. A check was finally drawn against her Chase Manhattan account in New York, and the sale was made.

"You will be happy with it," the owner assured her.

"I know I will."

Delivery date was scheduled for early December. "By then, I shall have been home for at least a week or two," Louisa said, and they left the shop a scant twenty minutes after they had gone in.

And now Paul Chandon is quite certain of her solvency, Iris thought, enraged. If he had any doubts before, he could have none now. The price of the clock had been in four figures, and it hadn't taken her aunt long to make up her mind.

Why must I have this cross to bear? she asked herself disconsolately. My first trip abroad…and this kind of thing has to happen.

And he was so charming. Smiling, casual, gallant…. Like some young *grand seigneur*…as if he owned the world, instead of being what he was, a shrewd, calculating chaser of rich, defenseless women.

"I will drop you somewhere," Paul announced, looking at his watch. "Wherever you wish to go from here."

"Let's see, it's almost four. What shall we do, Iris?"

"I haven't the slightest idea. It's a bit too late to do much, isn't it?"

"Well, we could go shopping. You wanted to buy some gifts."

"Very well, we'll go shopping."

"Paul, if you can find us a taxi. You have an appointment, so one for you and one for us. We'll go over to Trois Quartiers."

"Oh, but I don't like to—"

"My dear, we can certainly manage to get ourselves over to the stores," Louisa said. "Let's each take our own cab and call it a day. And a very pleasant day, thanks to you."

At last, with Paul solicitously helping them into one cab and flagging down another for himself, they said their final good-byes.

"My word," Louisa said, settling back in her seat. "Wasn't that nice. A lovely few hours on a lovely day."

"I don't see that we have much time left for shopping," Iris said sulkily.

"Oh yes, a good couple of hours. Enough time for you to find some pretty things to take home as presents. Oh, I shouldn't have bought that clock. Think of all the starving Armenians."

"That was a long time ago," Iris said, laughing in spite of herself. "Other people are starving now, Aunt Louisa. The Third World."

"I expect so. Life is so unfair. Oh, but I did enjoy this day. Lunch, a very *good* lunch, with someone as handsome and considerate as Paul."

"You do seem to like him."

"I think he's *delightful.*"

No kidding, Iris thought grimly, and wondered what, exactly, was going to come next.

The Roman Spring of Mrs. Stone, she thought gloomily. Only for Roman, substitute Parisian.

And for Mrs. Stone, substitute Mrs. Collinge.

Ten

"I've just made an appointment with the hairdresser," Louisa announced the next morning. "And then I had a call from friends of mine who live on the Faubourg St. Honoré. They've asked me for lunch. I told them my niece was with me, and they would like you to come, too."

"Oh dear, must I go?"

"No, you needn't, and as a matter of fact I didn't expect you'd want to, so I said you might like a day all to yourself and of course they understood."

"I'd love a day all to myself! That would really test my mettle. It's just the kind of challenge I need. You wouldn't mind, then?"

"Of course not. I'll be a couple of hours at the beauty salon, so my day is rather taken up as it is. I have no doubts at all that you'll manage beautifully. But remember, Paul is calling for us at five o'clock, so you had better be home not much later than four."

She swallowed her breakfast coffee hastily. "And now I must dash or I'll be late for my hairdresser."

She knocked on Iris's door before she left, and called in, "Have a nice day, won't you?"

"I will. You too."

"Bye now, darling."

When she was alone, and dressed for the street, Iris sat down to map an itinerary for her day's jaunt. There were dozens of places she wanted to go to, but as time would be somewhat limited, due to having dinner with that awful Paul Chandon tonight, she would have to plan rather carefully.

She got out her walking map, picking and choosing, always coming back to the fact that, because of that horrid dinner date this evening, she couldn't go to the Père Lachaise cemetery where the immortals of the ages were buried because she would want to spend hours there…and there wouldn't be time for that today.

Nor could she ferret out La Grande Jatte, because that would mean a long Metro ride and a lot of exploring in unknown territory.

What she really would like to do most would be to take a train to Chartres, which was only about two hours away, stay all day and return in the late evening.

Chartres…the cathedral of Chartres…

But she couldn't go there unless she skipped the dinner date with that miserable Paul Chandon…and if she did that, it would mean her aunt would be alone with him.

No way!

It was then that she had a perfectly ghastly thought.

Those friends of Louisa's, the ones on the Faubourg St. Honoré…the ones she was lunching with…anyway, said she was lunching with.

Or were they just an excuse? Was Louisa really going to the Faubourg St. Honoré for lunch? Was she *really?*

Or was she, instead, meeting that sinister Paul Chandon somewhere?

Was that why she had given her niece a day off?

Oh, dear God.

She got up and paced the room.

I must not jump to conclusions, she told herself.

She even considered leafing through her aunt's little address book, which must surely be on her bedside table. See if she could locate those friends of the Faubourg St. Honoré.

If she could, then on some pretext she could phone them. Say something like, "I forgot to tell my aunt that…"

Tell her what?

She sagged. Then rallied, as after all she was only a very young average girl who wanted to enjoy a day in a strange, magical city all on her own…and by God, she was going to!

After all, Aunt Louisa was a grown woman. She must have *some* sense, for heaven's sake.

I'll worry later, Iris told herself, and bent over the map again, this time resolutely limning out her next few hours.

Then she left the hotel and walked briskly over to the Place de la Concorde which, situated as it was in her near vicinity, had become for Iris the focal point from which she regarded the rest of the city.

At any rate, the Place de la Concorde was one of the most glorious spots in Paris, for at its center one had a view of almost all the great landmarks of the city. You could see, all the way down the Champs Elysées, the noble contours of the Arc de Triomphe. You could see the classic Greek facade of the Church of the Madeleine. You could see the Palais Bourbon and you could see the Eiffel Tower spearing the sky.

But because of the vehicular traffic, you couldn't stay for longer than a minute or two at the Place de la Concorde…unless you had a yen to land up in some hospital. So you left it rather quickly and moved on.

You moved on, perhaps—as Iris did today—to that great, quintessentially beautiful expanse of the Champs Elysées, and you waded through the early fallen leaves that were heralding autumn, and were relieved, if only temporarily, of niggling worries and pesky little doubts. The Champs Elysées, in the prelude of Fall, had a particular smell.

Smells so…so different, Iris thought, and sniffed. In fact, Paris itself had a faintly musky, faintly perfumed odor. Perhaps, Iris thought, it was the perfume of the past. All the long eras, merging together, and combining in this bittersweet, pungent redolence. Elusive, intoxicating…

There were, in great profusion, flowers, bushes, trees, hedges. There were ornate lampposts that probably Dumas and Balzac had leaned against. There were benches where people of all ages and all classes sat and turned their faces up to the sun. And there was the sun itself, burning high in the vast Paris sky.

After a while, at a large circular mall called the Rond-Point, these "Elysian Fields" became a street of commerce, with airline companies lining the avenue, and boutiques, restaurants, outdoor cafes and film palaces taking the place of its earlier peace and quiet. There was Fouquet's, over on the left side of the avenue, and after a bit the Plaza Athenée, a hotel much favored by Americans.

And just up ahead the Arch of Triumph, outlined against an almost cloudless sky…

It took Iris a while to learn that there was an underground passage leading to it. At first, contemplating the swift rush of traffic that streamed past as she stood on a corner, she despaired of ever reaching it.

Then a sympathetic Parisian, noting her perplexity, touched her arm and pointed to the left.

"*Oui,*" she said, finally comprehending. "*Oui. Merci.*"

She walked over to the entrance of the subterranean walkway, went down the long flight of steps and finally, at the end of the tunnel, walked out into daylight again.

She was now at the base of the Arch and, dead ahead, flickering with a warm and blood-red glow, was the Eternal Flame, at the very core and heart of the Arch itself.

She spent a solemn moment there and then went underground once more, to again arrive at the other side of the Etoile.

From the Etoile, the twelve avenues radiated outwards. The one Iris was bent on exploring was the Avenue Marceau, which in turn would take her to the Place de l'Alma, her first goal for the day.

It was at the Place de l'Alma that, at this very time of year, one of Iris's friends had gathered chestnuts. In Iris's room, at home in Manhattan, were four fat chestnuts which had been a gift from that friend.

It was her weekend pleasure to polish them with a soft rag, look at them afterwards with fond delight, and then put them back in the little faience bowl still another friend had brought her from the Midi of France.

Today, Iris had decided, she would garner some Parisian chestnuts herself. Chestnuts *she* would scoop up from the ground, a memento of her first trip to Paris.

It was a very pretty hike, with the Eiffel Tower always in sight to the left, and the Avenue Marceau was quiet and lovely, increasing in attractiveness with each step. There was an abundance of trees, a charming little park, and at last she was once again at the Avenue President Wilson…and only a stone's throw from where she had been two days ago.

Now the area opened up into a great, unbroken expanse just off the river, and the cobalt-blue sign, *Place de l'Alma,* told her she had reached her destination.

It was a pleasing sight, this riverside retreat, and rather like Gracie Square in Manhattan, or Sutton Place, though to Iris's eyes far more alluring, and infinitely more expansive. In the background handsome buildings rose; apartments, most likely.

That it was a posh district was readily evident, and in that respect also a kind of kissing cousin to the upper East Side purlieus. And while Iris would have chosen the Palais-Royal as a place to live in Paris, this would be, she decided, her second objective.

One could dream, couldn't one?

It was beautiful and peaceful to walk along the Seine in the shade of leafy trees, with the river scents, pungent and heady, drifting into one's nostrils. It was cool and verdant and beguiling, without the sound of street traffic dinning in one's ears.

A few nursemaids, starched and prim, were wheeling shiny baby buggies; children played placidly. A boat whistle sounded.

And there were chestnuts underfoot…chestnuts in profusion. But Iris was selective. They must be plump and firm and golden-brown, and most of them that lay scattered at the base of the trees were worm-eaten, dull-colored and squashed.

It took her quite a while to find half a dozen beautiful, fat, sumptuously-bronzed specimens to take back with her. Pleased and satisfied, she dropped them carefully into a plastic bag and put them away in her tote.

Then she sat down for a well-deserved rest on one of the many benches that lined the embankment, thinking of her next and last foray, which would occupy the whole of her afternoon.

It was in Montparnasse that she would while away the rest of the day. Magical Montparnasse, the old "Greenwich Village" of Paris.

She stretched out her legs and leaned back, settling herself comfortably. A delicious breeze riffled her hair, and the river, tranquil and gray-green, flowed on, hypnotic and lulling.

She closed her eyes, drinking in the glory of the day.

And dozed off.

A voice, very close to her, woke her with a start.

Opening her eyes, she was for a moment disoriented. Then, blinking a little in the bright sunlight, she saw that a gentleman somewhat past middle age was bending over her.

"*C'est le votre*, Mademoiselle?" the gentleman asked, holding up a tote bag.

Her tote bag which must have slid off her lap. "Oh, thank you," she said. "I seem to be always losing things these days. *Merci*, Monsieur."

He dangled the bag and then put it on the seat beside her. "You are American," he said delightedly. "Would you mind very much if I sat down too?"

"Oh, please do," she answered, and he promptly joined her on the bench.

"I guess I fell asleep," she said sheepishly.

"It's the kind of day to fall asleep," he consoled her. "I myself fall asleep often, without planning it. Sometimes, even standing up," he added, with a chuckle.

"I've been doing a lot of walking. Which takes its toll."

"It does indeed."

His accent was delicious, like melted butter, Iris thought. He had bright blue eyes, wore a navy beret, and seemed somewhere between fifty and fifty-five—about her own father's age.

He was different from her father, however. He was urbane, distinguished-looking and probably had been, Iris guessed, something of a ladies' man in his younger years.

Whereas her father was your typical American businessman, without a trace of this gentleman's European suavity. And she doubted that her father had ever been a swinger.

Yet she instantly knew that this man was not trying to attack her, make a play, or be an annoyance. He had been walking by, had seen her bag on the ground, and had made her aware of it.

You knew instinctively when a man had something nefarious on his mind. As you knew, just as instinctively, when he didn't.

This man would pass muster. She liked him right away. She wouldn't mind talking to him at all…in fact, she would very much enjoy it.

"Where do you live in the United States?" he asked her.

"New York City. Manhattan. Do you know New York, Monsieur?"

"Very well indeed. And I have many friends there. A most exciting city."

"A little worse for wear these days."

"Most of the large cities are a little the worse for wear. Here too." He smiled warmly, expectantly. "Is this your first glimpse of Paris?"

"Yes. And if you'd like my opinion of it, I can tell you that I'm madly in love with this city."

"Being in love with a city is a nice thing," he agreed, his eyes twinkling. "Are you in love in any other way?"

"You mean with a man? No. I was once…or I thought I was. But it didn't work out. That kind of love will have to wait."

"What a pity." His eyes swept over her, but not acquisitively. Appreciatively, yes…but there was no suggestion of lechery. This was not a dirty old man.

She said, dryly, "I still feel I have a little time."

His smile, which made small grooves around his blue eyes, agreed with her. "Oh, plenty of time," he concurred. "Only it makes me a little sorry. Being in love with someone makes the days seem so much shorter, don't you think so?"

"But I'm not sure I want the days to be shorter."

He nodded, and was a little wry. "It's a question of age," he said, and smiled again. "When you are my age, the days often seem too long. There is an old saying. The years fly by, but the days drag.'"

He slid down in his seat. "How long have you been here, Mademoiselle?"

"Five days."

"And what have you done with those five days? If you don't object to my asking."

"Not at all. Well, let's see. We're staying at a hotel on the Place Vendôme, so I know that part of the city. And then…well, the usual, I expect. Notre Dame, Palais de Chaillot, Eiffel Tower, the Opéra, Champs Elysées…"

He nodded. "As you say, the usual."

"But a lot more," she said defensively. "We went to the Ile St. Louis and had lunch at a very French bistro which was *not* the usual, Monsieur…and after that we went to St. Germain."

"Deux Magots, *naturellement.*"

"That's just the attitude *he* took," Iris said resentfully. "That you only go to St. Germain to get a snap of yourself at Deux Magots. And it isn't like that at all!"

Her companion sat up, and put a hand on her elbow. "You have left me somewhat behind," he said, shaking his head. "You must forgive me, but I am only an elderly Parisian to whom matters must be explained in unfragmented detail. Yes?"

He held up a finger. "There is you, Mademoiselle. And then there is a we. After that there is a he. I *know you*....you are sitting here beside me and you are very lovely to look at. But who is we and who is he?"

Then he leaned back again. "Tell me the whole thing from the beginning," he suggested, with such an adorable grin that Iris wanted to hug him.

How nice men could be when they weren't young and nasty.

"What's your name?" she asked, moving closer to him.

"I will tell you mine if you will tell me yours."

"I'm Iris Easton, of New York City."

"I am Claude Marchand of Paris, France."

He bowed ceremoniously. *"Enchanté,* Mademoiselle Iris."

"Enchantée, Monsieur Claude."

"And now that we have been properly introduced, proceed with your story," he bade her.

"I don't have much of a story," she said. "Except that, in a way, yes, there have been some complications. In short…well, I'm here with my aunt, who is a widow and not old. She's forty-six, to be exact."

"That seems quite young to me," the man said dryly. "Considering that I am considerably older."

"You don't look it."

"Thank you, Mademoiselle, I will leave you money in my will."

"I'd settle for some more perfect chestnuts."

"I beg your pardon?"

She showed him her cache of nuts. "These are the things that mean something to me," she confided. "Shall I get on with my story?"

"By all means."

"Well…so she and I are here together. Her husband died just over a year ago, and this is her first trip abroad without him. I'm her favorite. Which is a little silly, since I'm her only young relative. But we love each other dearly."

She paused. "I'm not boring you?"

"Far from it. What comes next?"

"We arrived, as I said, five days ago and started right out sightseeing. A wonderful first day. Then the second day started out just as auspiciously. We took a long, beautiful walk, starting from the Concorde, then went over to the Left Bank and up along the quays there, and at the Quai des Grand Augustins we went into some of the antique shops. Aunt Louisa has a lot of money and buys old things of value. Then, after we spent some time at the bookstalls, we went to a cafe on the Place St. Michel."

She paused again, this time for breath, and her companion remarked that so far it seemed quite pleasant but otherwise uneventful.

"So far," Iris agreed. "But at that sidewalk cafe, what do you suppose happened?"

"I can guess, but tell me," Monsieur Marchand said, an amused glint in his eyes.

"Oh, all right, so I was accosted. At least I wasn't pinched, the way they do in Italy."

"*I* was never pinched in Italy," he said.

"No, you probably did the pinching," she answered shyly.

"I never used such crude methods," he replied, and then laughed. "But my salad days are so long gone that I don't even remember what arts I did employ."

But he looked disappointed. "Is that all?" he asked.

"No, that's the way everything began."

And bit by bit, she told him the whole saga. First a play for herself, then her aunt, and an entire day spent with the pushy stranger.

"Then yesterday, lunch with him, and this evening *dinner* with him," she wound up. "She's very, very rich, and all that gold jewelry, the alligator handbag…and after all, she's only forty-six. Frankly, I'm worried."

And then, though she hadn't meant to, she confided that this morning her aunt had pleaded a luncheon engagement with friends…but that now she was fearful that it had been only a subterfuge.

"Do you suppose, instead, that she met *him* today?" she demanded.

Monsieur Marchand thought it all over. Finally he said, "You are afraid that this young man is attracted by your aunt's money, is that it?"

"Yes, of course."

He shrugged. "Possibly. Then again, it's also very possible that he is attracted to your aunt herself."

"But why?" Iris asked, bewildered. "After all, *I'm* so much nearer his age! Why would…"

He turned round in his seat and faced her. "What you mean," he said, "is why would a man prefer your aunt to yourself?"

"No," she cried. "I didn't mean that! I just meant…"

He didn't say anything more. He simply listened, and waited.

And after a while Iris slumped, dejected. Yes, she thought, lowering her eyes. That's exactly what she had thought. That instead of falling flat on his face for her, Paul Chandon had instead made his overtures to her aunt.

"Not that I wanted him to," she said at last. "I'm not in the habit of latching on to any man who…who…"

"I'm sure you're not," Claude Marchand said, patting her hand. "And I can understand that you are concerned about your aunt."

He gave her a warm, avuncular smile.

"You are a very pretty, and friendly, and candid young woman, and I have enjoyed this time together with you, Mademoiselle

Easton. I'm a little lonely these days, and a chance meeting with charming young American girls doesn't happen to me every day in the week."

He reached in his jacket pocket and pulled out a card case, from which he extracted a single piece of pasteboard.

"If you should ever be in trouble, or need a friend," he told her, "here is my address and telephone number. I live nearby here. Perhaps you will feel a little bit better if you know that there is someone you can depend on in an emergency."

He stood up, wished her a pleasant day and many other pleasant days, and said that now he was a little past due for a meeting with a colleague.

Then, with a little salute and a charming smile, he walked off and disappeared into the shrubbery beyond.

Iris put the card he had given her into her own card case, sat there for a few minutes longer, and got up. It was time to hie herself to Montparnasse for the next adventure.

She walked back the way she had come, up the Avenue Marceau, and found a Metro station near the Etoile. There was a map of Metro routes posted outside, which showed her which line to take and which station to get off, or substantially so. If she got off at the wrong station, at least it would be in the *arrondissement* she wanted.

And it was quite a little excitement to be riding the Paris subway. First one had to buy a ticket at a little booth, and Iris had trouble with what her aunt called the "yellow money," meaning the very small change. Centimes were a mystery even to Louisa, and she generally left all her "yellow money" behind with the room attendant, along with the customary tip.

It was decided for her, however, when she simply deposited a heap of centimes on the counter. The proper amount was taken and Iris was given her ticket.

After that there was another hassle. At the bottom of the stairs that led down to the train platform, a gate suddenly closed in front of Iris, trapping her behind it. A subway car came and went, and then the gate, as if by legerdemain, opened and freed her.

It was all great fun, and when she stepped out into daylight again, after getting off at Montparnasse-Bienvenue station, found herself in a section of the city teeming with activity.

It was a very warm day and rather humid, seeming to be about ten degrees hotter than where she had just come from, the riverside freshness of the Place de l'Alma.

It was an old district, of course…and in many places a bit seedy…but it was Montparnasse, with echoes of Hemingway and Scott Fitzgerald, and Picasso, Chagall and their ilk. This was hallowed soil to any lover of the arts and, like any lover of the arts Iris was bent on wandering about on streets that had known the footsteps of those she admired, of those who were now dead…but only in the flesh.

She was there for all of the hours remaining to her, reveling in the street names that evoked so much, and she had coffee at three celebrated cafes—the Dome, Coupole and Closérie des Lilas.

This meant a fair amount of footwork, and just as much time, so that when she had paid her check at the Closérie, and looked at her watch, she knew she would have to hurry in order to be back at the hotel in time to bathe and change for the evening's dinner in Montmartre.

She almost fell asleep on the Metro, and came near missing her stop. She walked the short distance to the Place Vendôme and to the hotel in a contented daze, congratulating herself on her success in doing it all without any help.

"Well, how did it go?" Louisa asked, when Iris arrived home.

"Fantastic. I even took the Metro."

Louisa laughed. "I knew you would."

"I went to—"

"Tell me later," her aunt said firmly. "It's way after four and you'll have to bathe and change as quickly as possible."

"Okay. How was your day?"

"Nothing exciting. Old and valued friends whom I always enjoy seeing, but it would have been boring for you."

Iris surveyed her aunt. The freshly-done hair, and with a touch-up, she noted. It was a good hairdo, very flattering, with a little swirl of hair over the forehead.

Aunt Louisa looked very pretty, very svelte, and very radiant. She didn't look as if she'd had a long, boring lunch with old and valued friends.

But I must not jump to conclusions, Iris told herself for the nth time, as she sat in the enormous tub and sprayed the hand shower over herself.

It was dangerous to have too lively an imagination.

But she wasn't looking forward to tonight. The three of them again, and then what?

Tomorrow again? The day after tomorrow…and so on, ad infinitum?

I do wish, she thought fervently, that we had never gone to that horrid little cafe on the Place St. Michel…and met that wretched Paul Chandon.

Eleven

It was unaccustomedly difficult, once Iris had stepped out of the shower, to get dressed and ready for her evening on the Butte. She got a dress and then changed her mind. No, not that one; it was too frou-frou, too girlish.

She riffled through the clothes in the big armoire and took out another one, eyeing it critically.

Impatiently, she put it back.

Damn it, what was she going to *wear?*

She went back, totally uncoordinated, to the bathroom, looked in the mirror and felt dissatisfied with her face.

Too much eyeshadow. And her hair didn't look right.

She took the hairbrush and attacked her hair again.

Then she wiped off some of the eyeshadow.

Now there was too little!

And what *dress* was she going to put on?

Oh, why weren't they going to some little restaurant nearby? Just she and her aunt. She felt bone tired, jumpy, and yearned for bed and a book.

The ring of the telephone almost jerked her off her feet.

Dear Lord, she thought, my nerves are in a terrible state.

She picked up the phone. "Hello," she snapped.

"I am sorry," the operator's voice said. "I meant to ring Madame Collinge's room."

"Yes…well, all right," Iris said, and almost knocked the phone off the bedside table hanging up the receiver.

She stood there in her bra and panties, considering. Maybe, she thought, maybe Paul Chandon was on the phone, saying that, after all, he was unable to have dinner with them.

Hope flared and then died. There was a knock on the door.

"Iris, nearly ready?" her aunt's voice called. "The desk just rang and said Paul's in the lobby."

So much for wild hopes, Iris thought, drooping.

"Nearly ready," she called back.

There was a silence. Then, "Are you coming out soon, dear?"

"Uh…you're all set to go?"

"Yes, and waiting for you."

Iris yanked open the door. "I'm sorry," she apologized. "Can you go down and keep him company? I'll try to hurry."

"Good heavens, look at you! Iris, *darling,* how long will you be?"

"Five minutes at the outside," her niece promised.

Her aunt looked doubtful.

"I'm all dressed, really. Just got to put something on and I'll be right down."

"Very well, then, I'll take him to the lounge. We'll have a quick aperitif. Join us there…but dear, do make it snappy."

"Yes, yes."

Somehow she got herself together and, breathing deeply because she so dreaded the thought of the evening ahead, she went out into the corridor, locked the door and, feeling like a sacrificial lamb, stoically went down the two flights of stairs to the lounge which was filled with people having drinks, so that the room was humming with conviviality. The Hotel Vendôme had no dining room, and the bar lounge was consequently a popular place for those who stayed there.

Iris stood just inside the doorway, looking for her aunt. She didn't spot her right away, but when she did, she stepped back sharply. Her aunt was there, all right, and so was Chandon. They were sitting at a far table, in a little corner by one of the windows. There was a drink in front of each, but they weren't sipping. They were smiling into each other's eyes, and Louisa's two hands were joined with Paul's hands across the table.

Paling, her breath coming in shallow gasps, Iris stared, her worst fears realized. Those two people, seemingly unaware of anyone else but each other, told the whole tale. It was so obvious!

For a moment she wanted to flee, go back to her room, just get away...

But she couldn't do that. She couldn't just leave her aunt in the hands of this lounge lizard, this beach boy type. She couldn't simply wash her hands of the whole business.

She squared her shoulders, cleared her throat, and walked purposefully forward. When she had managed to squeeze through a crowded table or two and reach the corner where Paul and her aunt were seated, they were no longer clasping hands. Her aunt was holding her liqueur glass and Paul was lighting a cigarette.

He got up immediately and pulled out a chair for Iris.

"*Bon soir,*" he said.

"*Bon soir.*"

"What took you so long?" Louisa wanted to know.

"Frankly, I was tired. I walked all over creation today."

"What will you have to drink, Mademoiselle?"

"Nothing, thanks."

"Oh, have some vermouth or something," her aunt urged.

"I'll wait until before dinner. I'd rather."

"You don't look tired," Paul Chandon commented. "In fact, you look bright-eyed and very, very chic in that lovely dress."

Iris's eyes surveyed him quickly. He was meticulously turned out, as opposed to the other two times she had seen him. He had on a handsomely-cut suit in a lightweight twill and also light in color, a silk shirt with a faint pin stripe and a tie that had probably set him back twenty-five or thirty dollars.

This Paul Chandon clearly had expensive tastes.

With his deep tan, dark hair and deepset eyes, he was a man any woman would look at more than twice.

And that was just the trouble. He was *too* good-looking, *too* dashing, *too* spectacular. Men that handsome found conquests just too easy…and were rarely to be trusted. This particular one wasn't to be trusted at all.

"Did you have a pleasant day?" he asked her. "I understand that you were left to your own devices."

"I had a lovely day, thank you."

"Good." He tossed off the rest of his drink. "Suppose I go downstairs and phone for a taxi at the desk. Then you can take your time and come down when you are ready."

"Fine," Louisa agreed. "We'll be right with you."

He stood up, gave one of his formal little bows, and strode off.

Louisa's eyes followed him. "Doesn't he look wonderful this evening," she murmured. "Don't you think he's a singularly attractive young man?"

"*Chacun à son gout,*" Iris said, forcing a smile.

"Iris, I…"

There was a small pause, while Iris waited warily. Her aunt had *such* an odd look on her face.

"Yes, Auntie?"

"I want you to have a good time tonight. I mean by that, I want you to have a superlative evening—an evening you'll remember."

She leaned forward. "We're going to one of the most bewitching spots in all Paris," she said softly. "The Place du Tertre. It's at the top of one of the city's seven hills, at the very crest of Paris. There's the cathedral, Sacré Coeur, white as white, like alabaster, and it's a kind of crown Paris wears. Say what you will about the dubiousness of its architecture, it's beautiful, bizarrely beautiful. And there's a rampart at its base, where you stand, looking down at the city, which at eventide is dusky, hushed, and…and everything seems to come to a kind of standstill."

Louisa's eyes were far-seeing, as if she were talking to herself. "Then," she said, "as the day darkens…rapidly now…a light winks on down below in that great city. And then another light. And another…and in the twinkling of an eye, that city down there is a great blaze of glory, as the lights go on all over Paris."

She looked earnestly into her niece's eyes. "I've seen that moving sight many, many times. But the first time you see it is the most meaningful, the most important. Never again will the impact be quite as thrilling. Always glorious, yes, but never, ever again as potent."

Louisa's eyes were shining…and part of the shimmer in them was from tears that lay behind them. But her voice, when she spoke again, was steady, and she smiled tenderly at Iris.

"I don't want anything, *anything* to interfere with this first time for you," she said. "For me, darling, put everything else aside. Everything. Just let yourself go. Let yourself *feel*. Let your eyes be your heart tonight. Will you do that for me?"

Touched to the quick, Iris nodded. "I will, of course I will," she promised. "And thank you, Auntie, for painting such a lovely picture. If you love it so, then so will I. You must realize that I've dreamed about this kind of beauty all my life."

"Then," Louisa said briskly, "shall we go?"

•••

The taxi wound through the streets of the city, fighting the heavy traffic and, at many corners, rounding them on two wheels…or so it seemed. Drivers leaned on their horns, and cab hackies cursed each other loudly at intersections.

Louisa, naturally, had climbed in first, then Iris, so that Paul Chandon was on the outside, at Iris's right. Whenever a sharp turn occurred, she and Paul were thrown together and he would say politely, "Sorry," as shoulders and legs brushed one against the other.

Grin and bear it, Iris bade herself, and sat stiffly, shunning the contact as best she could. On one side of her was the faint but pervasive smell of her aunt's perfume, and on the other, the slight whiff of Paul Chandon's shaving lotion, and the overall smell of him—his clothing, the Gauloise he had been smoking—and his maleness.

But she bore the ride with good grace. What her aunt had said in the lounge was still very much with her. She kept thinking that yes, of course, the first time Louisa had seen what they were going to see tonight and which she had described so beautifully, had been with Henry, on their honeymoon in France.

It had meant very much to Louisa, who wanted it to mean very much to her, Iris, and no matter how she felt about the status quo, tonight she was going to do what she had promised her aunt… relax and enjoy it. Put all other thoughts aside, and simply let her "first time" at the Place du Tertre be unforgettable.

For herself, the first time could have been on her own wedding trip. Mark Pawling had been long forgotten, shelved along with other useless things. What remained of that deplorable little interlude was only the shock…and the hurt. The man himself was only a dim and sad memory in her mind.

Paul suddenly leaned forward and told the cab driver that they would stop here, and the vehicle came to a grinding halt.

"We'll get out here," Paul explained to them, "and walk the rest of the way."

When they were standing on the sidewalk, he told Iris that he thought she might find this particular street of some interest.

It was a very hilly one, for it led up to the height of Montmartre, and on both sides of it were drygoods stores, one after another, with colorful fabrics displayed in their windows. It was very much like a street in the garment district of New York, and almost as congested.

"If you happened to be a girl who made her own clothes," Paul told Iris, "you would find many bargains here."

He looked down at her, smiling. "But I don't think you make your own clothes."

"No, I'm afraid I don't have the talent for it"

After a while, as they ascended slowly, they came to the seemingly endless flight of steps that led up to the Butte.

"Shall we walk up?" Paul asked.

"Of course we'll walk up. And when we leave we'll walk down," Louisa said gaily. "It's all part of the ambience."

"Then Madame, Mademoiselle…"

They started up the steep flight of stone steps. And after a while it became evident that there were houses clambering up the ascent. There was a wide space between the stairs and the houses, with rows of sheltering trees between, but there were occasional glimpses into rooms that were illumined by the sun that still lingered in early evening, and charming little domestic scenes within. A table laid for supper, a woman at a cookstove, a man reading a newspaper.

Three small boys, laden with gigantic loaves of bread like enormous cigars, came down the steps toward them, said shyly, "*Bon soir,*" and went on down past them.

"Those loaves of bread were almost as large as the children," Iris marveled.

"Those are *baguettes.* For the evening meal. Baked fresh every day," Paul said.

"Going up and down these steps must be a hazard in the wintertime," Iris commented. "With snow and ice. I wouldn't want to take my chances."

"Oh, but it is great fun for children. Sometimes they can slide down, when the ice forms a solid sheet."

He looked down at her. "Paris is, I sometimes think, at its best in the cold months. Then there are no tourists about at all, and Paris belongs to the Parisians again."

"I suppose we *are* a bother," she said tartly, and he laughed.

"Some are, but certainly not the company in which I find myself," he said, and for a brief moment touched her arm.

Iris resisted an impulse to pull away from his touch, or look down pointedly at his hand on her. But remembering the promise to her aunt, she smiled nicely…and in any event, the hand didn't rest there for very long.

At last they were at the top.

There, looking like all the countless pictures she had seen of it, was Sacré Coeur, in its field of green lawn and, as Aunt Louisa had said, as white as alabaster.

They walked the distance over to the parapet. "Now we'll just stand here and wait," Louisa said. "And Iris, darling, it is worth waiting for."

It was a few minutes before seven, and on this early September evening the sky was still brilliant, but slowly gathering the colors of the coming night. The sun had set but, as it died, spread the vestiges of its radiance throughout the great expanse of sky that covered Paris. Little by little the flame and vivid pinks became softer, more diffuse, turning to gentle violets and darker purples.

And at last, as if a giant hand had snuffed out the day, it was evening.

"Watch now," Louisa said softly.

There was at first only a shadowy, mysterious city down below, with no more nuances of color in the sky. In the deepening dusk, all seemed muted and waiting, as if time itself had been arrested… until suddenly, eerily, there was a pinpoint of brightness down below…like the flick of a match.

And then a city, which had been nearly invisible a few seconds before, was incandescent with light. Night-time Paris had come to life.

"It's all right," Louisa said gently. "I cried too, the first time."

Twelve

The Place du Tertre, that traditional haven for painters, was now empty of them. Palettes and brushes had been put away for the day, and the great outdoor restaurant, with its seemingly limitless rows of umbrellaed tables, all lit with small, rosy lamps, was like a festival in the darkness.

"This is really something," Iris exclaimed, overwhelmed. "It's all like a great, fantastic party!"

"Europeans like the open air," Louisa said, "as you can readily tell from their streetside cafes."

"Yes, and I think it's marvelous."

They were led to a table on the border of the area, which gave them a measure of privacy. It also afforded a view of the night sky, where they could see the stars that were appearing overhead.

"I'll have a *very* dry martini," Iris announced. "I am quite undone by that incredible transformation we just saw…the lights going on all over the city. Oh, don't look at me! I still feel like bawling."

"Only someone with a heart of stone would fail to vibrate to it," Louisa agreed. "Paul, a martini for me too, please."

"*Deux martinis, très sec, et pour moi un Dubonnet blonde,*" he told the waitress.

"*Merci, Monsieur,*" the girl said, with a flirtatious, red-lipped smile. She was young, pretty and with a rather shocking cleavage.

It was all enormously festive and exciting and Iris, as she had promised, sat back and allowed herself to enjoy the delightful surroundings to the full.

It was certainly romantic, with the sparkle of crystal and silver on damask cloths, the winking radiance of the little table lamps and the riot of color the rows of overhead umbrellas provided.

A strolling violinist, clad in Romany garb and very dashing, played songs of yesterday and today. He played well, and the music added its bit to the overall effect. Occasionally someone sang a few bars along with the violin.

The martini, when delivered, was excellent, dry and bracing. "It's perfect," Iris said gratefully.

"So is mine," Louisa declared, and all three of them clinked glasses with cheerful abandon.

To sit up here at the top of Paris, under the darkening sky, midst the rows and rows of tables that made tiny little islands, was like being separated from the rest of the world, totally removed from reality. The soft glow of the lamps which—as far as the eye could see—lit the dark of the Montmartre night, was almost hypnotic.

The shadowy street that surrounded the large central area of the outdoor restaurant seemed to pulse with recollections of things past. It was easy to imagine that, tired after a day's painting, Utrillo, lugging his artist's paraphernalia, was heading for the steps they had earlier climbed. Or Vlaminck, not yet famous, was on his way home to a spare meal of bread and cheese.

"What are you thinking of?" Paul asked Iris.

"Lots of things…all very nice."

"My thoughts are nice too," he said, and gave her a teasing look. "Of course I am thinking of pretty ladies, whereas you are undoubtedly thinking about—"

"You think your thoughts and I'll think mine," she retorted, smiling. "*I* was thinking about how much I love Paris."

"Very commendable," he said. "So do I."

He hummed a few bars of the song, and before she knew it, Iris was humming too. At which Paul picked up the words.

"I love Paris in the winter, when it drizzles," he sang and Iris, chiming in, added, "I love Paris every moment…every moment of the year…"

And then, quite carried away, she finished the song with him.

"That was charming," Louisa cried. "Both of you have such beautiful voices. As for me, I can't even carry a tune. And Paul, your taking the second part, the harmony, was really lovely."

"One of my few gifts," he said, with a flashing smile. "Is everyone ready for another drink?"

Iris, when the second martini was brought to her, thought that she was having no trouble keeping her promise to her aunt. It was impossible, under the circumstances, to feel anything but joyous in such a beguiling setting and on such a balmy night.

She felt like dancing, like getting up on the table and dancing. She felt like filling one of her shoes with champagne and handing it out for all to drink from.

She was brought out of this reckless reverie by the violinist standing at their table. He threw a white-toothed smile Iris's way, bowed gracefully, and asked what she would like him to play.

"Oh dear," she said, drawing a blank. She couldn't think of anything but *Autumn Leaves,* and Parisians must be sick and tired of that old chestnut.

"Please…you decide," she said to Paul.

"Very well," he said, and after thinking for only a moment, told the man, *"Toujours je t'aime, chérie."*

It was one of the *very* sentimental songs, and the musician played it soulfully, his eyes first on Iris, then Paul.

Iris, acutely embarrassed, toyed with her bracelet. She could have killed Paul Chandon for his ill-chosen selection. It was only natural that the violinist would assume that the two younger people were attached to each other.

Couldn't Paul have realized what would happen? And how must her aunt feel about this ridiculous mistake?

She felt that there would be no end to it. With melting cadenzas and little trills, the violinist wrung the last drop of poignancy from the song, until Iris's nerve ends were thoroughly frazzled.

At last he finished, with a final flourish of the bow across the strings. Then he clicked his heels together and made a sweeping bow.

"*Merci,*" Paul said, and put a bill in his hand.

"*Merci, Mesdames, Monsieur,*" the man said, and with another bow, moved on.

"Iris, we must thank Paul for choosing that beautiful piece," Louisa said, and to Iris's relief she didn't look the slightest bit put out.

"Thank you," Iris said obediently.

"It's always been a favorite of mine," Louisa confessed. "Though I haven't heard it in years."

"Is it a favorite of yours?" he asked Iris.

"Oh, you can't beat these unabashedly sentimental numbers for a heart tug or two," she answered carelessly. And then because he looked really hurt and suddenly rather vulnerable, she added, "I like it very much and I heard it only recently, in New York."

"Where?" her aunt wanted to know.

"At the Hotel Meurice. They have a Continental restaurant I'm fond of. A girl with a really good soprano voice sang it. Incidentally, that man is very good on his instrument."

"He's probably a student at the Conservatoire."

The next song played, to Iris's amusement, was *Autumn Leaves*. There must be still a few Americans left in Paris, she decided.

"Well, I suppose we should think about ordering," Louisa said, and Paul signalled for the menus.

Louisa only glanced at hers. "Escargots, of course."

"And for me as well," Paul said. "Mademoiselle?"

"Thank you, but no."

"An unadventurous palate?"

"In this case a squeamish one."

"Perhaps some day you will change your mind."

"I don't forsee it, but anything's possible."

"Yes," he said. "As you say, Mademoiselle, anything is possible."

The constant "Mademoiselle" grated on her nerves. If I hear it one more time, Iris thought, I'll have a fit.

"You know my name," she said to him. "I realize that Europeans are a lot more formal—and to my mind somewhat stilted—than we are. My name is Iris. Is there any reason why you can't say that instead of Mademoiselle?"

"No reason at all," he replied. "I wondered why you had not suggested it before."

"Was I supposed to suggest it?"

"Different cultures have different customs, Iris."

"I won't dispute that, Paul." She smiled. "I'll have gigot, please."

With the meal, Paul chose a hearty red wine that would, he told them, go well with snails as well as the lamb.

The violinist played, the breeze sighed through the trees, and the lamps cast their subdued radiance. There was little conversation after a while: all three of them simply sat back and reveled in the beauty of the night.

They lingered over their meal for a long time. And after their coffee and dessert, Paul suggested brandy.

"Yes, that would be nice," Louisa agreed.

"I simply *can't,*" Iris protested.

They had polished off the bottle of wine, which now nestled in its ice bucket drained to the last drop.

Also, two martinis before that.

"Yes, you can," Louisa said. "It will settle your tummy after that hearty meal."

The waitress sashayed over.

"*Trois fines,*" Paul told her. "*Et l'addition, s'il vous plaît.*"

"*Oui oui, Monsieur.*"

"You French do like your firewater," Iris commented. "All the time wine, cognac, brandy…"

"You Americans drink cocktails, we don't," he reminded her. "Try and get a martini, for example, at the average cafe. You won't. They are served only where tourists go."

He flicked his lighter for Louisa's cigarette, and then pulled one of his Gauloises from a pack. The waitress brought their brandies, and Paul warmed his with his fingers caressing the tumbler.

"But you are right about the wine," he admitted. "In many parts of Europe, as you certainly know, the water is not quite up to snuff. And also not as plentiful as in your country."

"And so," he went on, "we drink wine. Many French schoolchildren have, in their lunchboxes, their *tartine*, their cookie, and a half liter of wine."

"Don't you think that's a bit dangerous?"

"You mean it will make small drunkards out of them?" He shook his head. "Not at all. The familiar is not a danger. It is the forbidden that is tempting…and that leads to overindulgence."

"Perhaps."

They prepared to leave at a little after ten-thirty. Many of the tables had been vacated, and the violinist had packed his instrument away and departed.

"Must we go?" Iris murmured. "Can't we stay a little longer… say about twenty years?"

"In twenty years, you'll be forty-four, and life would have passed you by still sitting here in the Place du Tertre."

"I'm not sure I'd mind."

The check was paid by Paul, quickly and unobtrusively, even before Louisa noticed that it had been brought. Afterward, she protested that it was totally unfair, that he was to have been *her* guest tonight. He was a very naughty boy, she said, and what was she going to *do* about him?

For a brief moment Iris felt a grudging respect for Paul Chandon. He had handled the ticklish matter with a certain aplomb.

And then she told herself that after all it was an investment on his part; an investment that could pay off handsomely if he played his cards right. A couple of lunches and a dinner amounted to very little if the stakes were high enough.

But she resolutely declined to dwell on it. She had promised to be a good girl, enjoy her evening, and make this a night to remember. And she would damned well keep her promise.

Besides, she felt much too contented to mull over unpleasant matters. It *had* been a wonderful evening, and she *had* enjoyed it…one hundred percent.

When they finally rose to go, she was a bit unsteady on her feet. Too much booze…she should never have had that brandy. Yet this had been a banner evening, and what did it matter in the general scheme of things if she was a little bit pie-eyed?

When they made their way back to the long, steep flight of steps leading down to the street, Louisa drew back.

"I've just decided," she said, "that I'll take the elevator instead."

"Elevator?" Iris demanded. "What do you mean, elevator?"

"There is one, and I shall take it."

"Then we'll all take it."

"No, no, you must walk down," Louisa insisted. "You and Paul take the stairs, and I'll meet you at the bottom."

Iris looked down. "There are more now than when we came up," she objected.

"Same number," her aunt said cheerfully. "And you must do it right, go down the same way you came up. It's all," she said airily, "part of an evening on the Butte."

She waved them on, and walked away.

"Why don't we take the elevator, too?" Iris suggested to Paul. "It's pretty dark down there now."

"I won't let you be mugged," he reassured her. "So no need to worry."

"Mugged? Where do you get those American phrases?"

"From girls like you," he said casually.

"I'll bet," she retorted. "And women like my aunt."

He nodded. "And women like your aunt." "Yes, I'm sure there are always one or two around," she flashed back.

"Steady there…"

She had stumbled, and now moved closer to the railing at her left.

"Need some help?" Paul asked.

"If I do, I'll whistle."

"Oh, you whistle too? By the way, you do have a nice voice, as your aunt said. You really should study with a good teacher. You still have the head tones of someone very young."

"But then, as you pointed out on another occasion, I *am* someone very young," she answered to that.

"True."

"An ingenue."

In the dim light his smile, amused and tolerant, flashed.

"Just someone very young," he said.

"And you prefer a woman a bit more…shall we say, seasoned?" she asked, challengingly.

"I prefer a woman who is warm, responsive, and—"

And rich? she was about to add, but caught herself in time. She had behaved very well and she wasn't going to spoil it now. Not tonight, at any rate.

On the next flight she stumbled again.

"Having trouble?" Paul asked.

"It's just that I drank too much. I should never have had that damned brandy."

"You should never have had those damned martinis," he corrected her.

"They're what I'm accustomed to, thank you. Whereas, brandy's not. And you and I had most of the wine."

"Wine won't hurt you."

"Too much of it will."

"Too many martinis will, if you don't mind my saying so."

"I do mind. How many flights are there left?"

"Four more."

"I can't make it," she said flatly, and sat down on one of the steps.

"Shall I carry you down?"

"If you do, I'll report you to the police."

"For what reason?"

"Making unwelcome advances."

"No danger of that."

"Why? Am I so repulsive?"

"You are beautiful," he said. "Very beautiful. But also *noli me tangere*. Look, but do not touch. I have left my reckless twenties behind, Iris, and along with it, *les jeunes filles*."

"You really are an impossible person," she cried, jumping up. "And if you refer to me as a little girl one more time, I'll—"

"Yes?" he said interestedly. "You will do what?"

"Never mind," she flung at him, and started running down the steps.

He ran down after her. "You will break a leg," he cried.

At the bottom she was breathless. He caught up to her. "You certainly can run," he said admiringly.

"Where," she demanded, "is that elevator?"

"Right over this way," he said, and they walked a short distance to where, along with several other people, Aunt Louisa stood waiting.

"Got down all right, I see," she commented.

"Except that your niece almost fell once or twice," Paul remarked. "However, I took good care of her. Well, shall we take a little stroll through Pigalle?"

"Thank you, no," Louisa replied. "I don't relish getting hit over the head by some Pigalle thug."

"Discretion is the better part of valor in this vicinity," he agreed. "There's a taxi stand just up ahead."

The group of people with whom Louisa had been waiting seemed happy about the taxi stand. They were, clearly, late American tourists, and in this poorly-lit street that seemed to go nowhere, no one could blame them for being uneasy.

So that, along with the three of them, there were also half a dozen patrons of the restaurant on the hill trooping toward the cab stand.

Paul, like a proper host of the city, saw that all of them were accommodated before he flashed a cab for themselves.

"That was thoughtful of you," Louisa said. "It's so dark at the foot of the Butte. They were all absolutely terrified."

During the ride back, the song that had been played for their table was running through Iris's mind. She was, at first idly and then doggedly, trying to remember the words. She had heard it only a few months ago, and recalled that she had been humming it at odd moments for days afterwards.

The melody was, admittedly, haunting, though the words were sickish sweet and mushy…too much so for her to waste time trying to bring them to mind.

All she could dredge up now were the first and second lines.

> *Toujours je t'aime chérie*
> *Always, my love, forever*

She sang the tune in her mind, but the rest of the words eluded her.

She was so preoccupied that her aunt had to ask her a question twice before she came to with a start.

"I beg your pardon?"

"I asked if you'd fallen asleep," Louisa said. "You're so quiet."

"I was just thinking of what a good time we just had."

"I'm glad. I hoped you would."

They said their good-nights in front of the hotel. "It was an evening to remember," Paul murmured, holding Louisa's hand and then raising it to his lips.

"It was for me," she said. "It was just the way I wanted it to be, Paul."

"I think," he answered, in a voice so low that the words were almost indistinguishable to Iris, "it was the way I wanted it to be."

The cryptic words, from both her aunt and Paul, sent a chill up Iris's spine. What did they mean? Or at any rate, what did Paul's mean?

Her aunt had wanted her, very much, to have a memorable evening. That would explain what Louisa had said.

But Paul?

I think it was the way I wanted it to be...

In the next moment her own hand was in Paul's. His mouth grazed it, then he let it go.

"Good night, Iris," he said. "Sleep well."

With a wave to them both, he climbed back into the waiting taxi, which drove away with a rev of its motor and a spit of backfire.

"That was a truly super gala evening," Iris said when they were in their quarters. "And Aunt Louisa, I assure you, one I won't forget. It was a hundred percent perfect."

"I did want it to be," Louisa said. "I did so much want it to be."

She gave Iris a quick hug and then suggested that they both immediately turn in. "So that we won't be too fagged out to have fun tomorrow."

"Good night, Auntie."

"Good night, darling."

There were many things to think about, but the day's activities, and then the magical evening just past—combined with martinis, Pommard and brandy—sent Iris spinning off to sleep almost as soon as she laid her head on the two fat pillows.

But in the morning she woke with that damnable song of the night before running through her mind. *"Toujours je t'aime chérie…"*Or in plain English, "I'll love you always, dear…"

> *I'll love you always, dear*
> *Always, my love, forever…*

Oh, stop it, she told herself. Once you tried to track down something that lay buried in your brain, it nagged at you, *nagged* at you!

It was in the shower that the next two lines popped into her head.

> *Awaking, aching am I*
> *For lips that haunted my dreams…*
> *Da da da da da da da…*

I will not think about it again, she told herself and, with a great effort of will, closed off that part of her mind and concentrated on her ablutions.

And she didn't think about it. Not consciously, at any rate. But her subconscious had, all on its own, apparently been busy working away, for as she was giving her hair a final brush, another line burst forth, like Minerva out of Zeus's forehead.

> *With feverish joy and gladness.*

She stood in front of the mirror, her hairbrush arrested, and sang softly.

> *Toujours je t'aime chérie*
> *Always, my love, forever*
> *Awaking, aching am I*

For lips that haunted my dreams
With feverish joy and gladness...

Or something like that...and near enough.

I do have a nice voice, she thought and then, throwing down the brush and insisting to herself that she would not think about dumb song again, grinned at her reflection and, opening her door, went into the salon for her "continental breakfast."

Thirteen

"*Good* morning," Louisa said, from the depths of the Recamier sofa. "How about going to Versailles today?"

"Oh, fantastic, let's do."

"It will take the whole of the day, of course. You don't go to Versailles for a quick half hour. There's much to see there, as I'm sure you can imagine."

"Time isn't really of the essence, though, is it? We have days and days ahead of us."

Louisa looked thoughtful. "Well," she said slowly, "we've been here almost a week, and there are other places to visit in France. How about taking a flight…say, the day after tomorrow, to the Riviera?"

"You mean leave Paris so soon?" Iris asked blankly.

"You have only three weeks," her aunt pointed out. "I was thinking of spending a week on the Côte d'Azur and after that a few days in the Provence. We could plan it so that you'd have your last couple of days back in Paris again."

"Well…I just—"

"Believe me, the Côte d'Azur is beautiful. Nice, Cannes, Villefranche, Monte Carlo…"

"Oh, I'm sure it's wonderful."

"And at this time of year no longer honky tonk, as it certainly can be in high season."

"The only thing is, there are reams of things I still haven't seen here. And I know it's touristy, but I did want to sail around on the Bateau Mouche."

"If you like, we can skip the Provence, and give you a whole additional week here before you leave for home."

Leave for home…

A pang wrenched at Iris's heart. How quickly the days had gone! It had seemed like an endless time to spend in France…but already six of the precious days were gone, if one included today.

And some day she would have to leave for home.

"Besides," her aunt went on, "if we leave day after tomorrow, you'll have an entire day in between, to do what you like. We can get in a lot of those things you mentioned."

"Yes, of course."

But the thought of leaving Paris was simply heartbreaking. Even for the French Riviera. And even though Paul Chandon had been a fly in the ointment…still, to say good-bye, even for a little while, to the City of Light.

"Well, what do you think, Iris?"

"Sure, Auntie. Yes, you're right, and I know I'll love the Côte d'Azur and the Mediterranean. It would be silly not to take advantage of it."

"Then if that's settled, I'll have the concierge make our flight and hotel bookings."

She rose briskly. "And now I must dress and go down to make all the arrangements before we leave for Versailles. You'd better get ready too."

"Yes, sure."

But Iris sipped her coffee listlessly, feeling unaccountably out of sorts. Only today and tomorrow left in Paris…and then so long. Only today and tomorrow…

Even if they returned, for another full week, it wouldn't be the same. She would have to orient herself all over again.

Yet her aunt's heart was clearly set on treating her to the lush and luxurious playground of the idle rich, providing her with further splendors.

A week ago she would have been overjoyed to be taken to the Riviera. But that was before she fell so wholeheartedly in love with Paris. Now it seemed, somehow, like a tragic loss, almost a punishment.

It was funny about Paul Chandon too, Iris thought. That her aunt didn't seem one bit upset about parting from him. And now she was planning to leave Paris, and leave Paul, for other localities…and more or less immediately. That seemed very odd, unless the glow had worn off. Unless Aunt Louisa had come to her senses…acknowledged the fact that she was being girlish and undignified and, having come to terms with herself about it, wanted to put Paul Chandon, and whatever he had come to mean to her, out of her mind…and sight.

Perversely, Iris felt a little sorry for Paul. Whatever he might be, whatever his intentions were, his plans had fallen through.

Besides, Paul wasn't so bad, when it came right down to it. He was undoubtedly a hanger-on, one of those European men who sized up older American women for gain and profit—what her mother would call a gigolo—but he didn't seem an evil person, an out and out rotter. She disapproved heartily of men like Paul, of course. But even Iris had to acknowledge, however reluctantly, his appeal.

He was a handsome animal…and his animal magnetism was all too potent. Why, she herself had felt it last night, when they went down the steps, alone together, after leaving the Place du Tertre. She had been a little provocative with him, as a matter of fact.

Not that it had encouraged him.

She had said something about calling the police if he made "unwelcome advances." *That* had been unpremeditated, and she had surprised herself.

He had only answered, however, that there was "no danger of it."

He was wily, certainly. Even if she held a certain attraction for him—which she obviously didn't—he wouldn't dare do or say anything that would endanger his relationship with her aunt.

Well, anyway, the situation had changed. They would be taking a flight to the south of France and Paul Chandon would have to shop around for another susceptible woman of indeterminate age.

We did have such a wonderful time last night, Iris thought pensively. Way up there on the Butte, with the soft breezes and the music, the starry night and the headiness of it all.

And that violinist thought she and Paul were lovers…

What would it be like to wander about Paris with a lover?

Like heaven itself, she thought. Like heaven itself.

Her aunt came out of her room fully dressed. "Why, Iris, you haven't budged from that chair! What's wrong with you?"

"Half an hour and I'll be ready to go," Iris said, getting up hastily. "Just a quick shower and into a pants suit."

Louisa sighed. "All right, meet me in the lobby. I'll go down now and give instructions about our flight on Wednesday. It shouldn't be too difficult to get rooms at the Negresco. But do hurry, dear, it's almost ten o'clock." At the door she waved. "Half an hour, mind."

"You've got it."

• • •

To get to the Chateau de Versailles, one took a little train and rode through a typical French countryside for an hour or so. At the end of that time one was in a small village which seemed strangely unfitting for the magnificent country residence that had once housed one of the most glittering royal courts in the world.

But as Iris and her aunt made their way along a bucolic little street and at last came to a spot where the palace stood behind a massive iron railing that was encrusted with gleaming gilt, it was instantly evident that here was the gateway of one of the illustrious structures of the ages.

Two ponderous gates, parted and layered almost from top to bottom with gold leaf, stood open, and the thunder of horsemen galloping through them seemed more like reality than imagination.

Three kings had lived here, of whom the ill-fated Louis XVI had been the last, and the only one to die a violent death, along with his pretty, feather-headed wife Marie Antoinette. In this place pleasure and debauchery had impoverished the National Treasury, as huge expenditures of francs and gold pieces ran through the hands of King, courtiers and mistresses like sand sifting through an hourglass.

Until the starving masses of France rose in revolt. On October 26, in the year 1879, the great days of Versailles were over. The mobs seized the palace and occupied it. The royal family was taken into custody, and the grim shadow of the guillotine lay over the last Louis to reign there.

The Revolution, though it destroyed many palaces, spared this one, and it was undoubtedly the most important such monument in Europe, and in the world. With its Le Notre gardens, its splashing fountains, its statuary, its enormous dimensions—2000 feet long—and the overall grace and refinement of its proportions, it presented a picture of unparalleled beauty.

"It's almost as if there was nothing but that incomparable facade," Iris breathed. "Or as if it were painted on the sky."

"Versailles, like Venice, has to be seen to be disbelieved," her aunt said.

She laughed good-naturedly when Iris began taking pictures. "Postcards will give you better shots, Iris."

"I know, but it isn't the same."

The interior, of course, was a storehouse of riches. The royal bedchambers, the chapel, the Queen's Staircase, the endless portraits, including Vanloo's painting of the Sun King, were delights to engage the imagination, and the Hall of Mirrors, where the treaties of two World Wars had been signed, was a place in which to ponder more recent history. The Hall of Mirrors held many secrets.

Outside once more, this time at the rear of the palace, were terraces, tree-shaded walks lined with statues; the vast acres of Versailles spread out for tourists now, its former hedonistic tenantry long dust.

"What next?" Louisa asked Iris.

"The Petit Trianon, of course."

And of course Louisa, the complete traveler, knew where it was, and they found the place where Marie Antoinette played at being *"une petite bergère"* easily enough.

It was open from two until five, for a fee of three francs, and as it was just short of three-thirty when they reached it there was plenty of time to explore.

So this was where the little German princess came to escape from the routine of court life, Iris mused. Where she put aside the pomp and the circumstance and, in these tranquil surroundings, felt—if only for brief periods—like any pretty, untroubled young girl.

Just a *jeune fille ordinaire…*

Paul Chandon's words echoed in Iris's mind. "Ingenues, not quite grown…"

What happened to men like Paul Chandon? What happened to them when they were old, no longer handsome, no longer virile.

And when even middle-aged women were no longer interested.

"If you want to see the Grand Trianon, we'll have to hurry," Louisa finally said.

"No, I won't bother. I'd really like to stay here until it closes," Iris said. "I don't know…somehow this place seems to have a special meaning for me."

"You once had a doll, which incidentally I gave you, whom you named Marie Antoinette. Do you remember?"

"I remember very well. It was a beautiful doll, bisque, with a lovely flower face and I think real hair that I brushed every day. I've always had a fondness for that winsome, pathetic queen, and I almost feel I've met her, being here."

• • •

The ride back on the chugging little train got them to the station at a little after seven. It had been a most bemusing day, and one that had made Iris reflective, even pensive. For the first time she regretted that their hotel had no restaurant. The thought of hastily changing for dinner and then trudging out somewhere was infinitely distasteful.

Apparently her aunt felt the same way.

"Instead of making a production about dinner," Louisa said, as they got into a taxi outside the station, "why don't we simply go to the King Charles just as we are, tired and crumpled. And then early to bed, I'd say."

"Super," Iris said gratefully. "I'll have their onion soup and then just some little thing."

Nor did they spend much time at the restaurant. Each ordered a simple meal and after their coffee they left and walked the short distance back to the Vendôme.

At the desk, the concierge was absent. Louisa rang the small silver bell, but there was still no sign of him.

"There's mail in our box," she said. "Iris, would you mind waiting until Guy comes? He'll have a message about our flight, too. I simply must go up and get out of these shoes."

"Okay, you go on up. I'll do the necessary."

Finally the concierge returned. "I am so sorry," he apologized. "A little trouble with a maintenance problem."

He reached in their box and pulled out a letter and some messages. The letter was for Iris. The messages, she saw, were for

Louisa. A glance at them showed that they were all from someone named Kitty, apparently one of Louisa's many friends, who seemed to have phoned at eleven o'clock, twelve o'clock and again at three. Kitty whoever-she-was had left a telephone number for Louisa to call.

"And will you tell Madame Collinge that the flight to Nice is confirmed," the concierge said. "A three o'clock departure. Also two single rooms with bath at the Negresco Hotel have been reserved."

"Thank you, I'll tell her."

"You had a pleasant day, Mademoiselle?"

"Very. We went to Versailles."

"You must go to Versailles at night too," he said. "For the *Son et Lumière*."

"I hope to, Guy. But that will have to wait until our return to Paris."

Then she remembered. "Oh yes, I must cash some traveler's checks."

"Certainly, Mademoiselle."

She tore three twenty dollar ones from her book of checks and signed them, but the concierge was interrupted by the ring of his phone before he could cash the checks for her.

"Excuse me," he said, and answered.

Iris leaned her elbows on the counter and waited while he said hello, and then made a connection.

When he hung up he said, smiling, "That was for Madame, your aunt."

It's probably the friend who's been calling her all day, Iris thought, as the concierge handed her some paper money and a few coins.

"Thanks and good-night," she said. "And now to bed."

"So early, Mademoiselle?"

"It was a long and tiring day, Guy."

When she let herself in the suite, her aunt was not in the salon. Her bedroom door was closed, and Iris decided to slip her friend's messages under the door.

She could hear Louisa's voice on the phone and had just stooped to slide the three slips of paper under the door when she heard her aunt say, "Yes, of course, Paul, but—"

Eavesdropping was not one of Iris's vices. But the next words electrified her. "Our flight's day after tomorrow, so you'd better wait at least another day. You could take a Wednesday flight."

It seemed to Iris that her heart had completely turned over. First a big leap in her chest, and then what was like a complete revolution. Her mouth fell open, and she was aware of that too.

After that, she listened shamelessly.

Some of her aunt's words were lost to her, so that only fragments of the conversation were clear. But the burden of the whole thing was accessible enough.

"The Negresco…"

"Yes, Paul, it's a risk…"

"You can only carry coincidence so far…"

Then a long silence.

Iris, stunned, fled to her room.

She tried to think, but all her thoughts were jumbled together. She felt paralyzed, unable to move.

So it had come to this…*he* was going too…Paul was following her aunt to the Côte d'Azur.

What else could those words mean? *"You'd better wait at least another day…it's a risk…"*

And…

How *awful* this was…how sordid…that her aunt would…

I can't *bear* it, she thought…that's he's really as bad as I thought. Paul Chandon, who quoted Dickens, and liked the Quai d'Orleans in the very early morning, and for whom she had been feeling sorry because she thought he was going to be left in the lurch.

She heard her aunt's door open and her name called out. Then a knock at her door.

She took a deep breath and walked across the room. Another deep breath, and then she opened the door.

"Hi," Louisa said, and saw the letter and the three slips of paper still in Iris's hand.

"Anything for me?" she asked.

"Yes, some phone messages. Here they are."

"Oh, good," Louisa said, scanning them. "Kitty and Jim. We had promised to meet if our paths crossed. Yes, I'll give her a ring right away."

She looked a little bit upset. "The only thing is…do you think you could manage another day alone tomorrow? I'd like to spend some time with them. What do you think…is it selfish of me?"

It was like a reprieve…that she wouldn't have to be with her aunt all day tomorrow, knowing what she knew. That everything she had feared was true, that Paul Chandon and her aunt were lovers…or planned to be.

Relief swept over her. Now she would have time to think, think what to *do!*

It made it easier for Iris to act naturally, tell Louisa that yes, she would be overjoyed to come and go as she pleased tomorrow and that yes, the flight to Nice had been confirmed and departure time was at three in the afternoon.

"And the hotel?"

"Also okay. Two singles with bath."

"Wonderful. We seem to be all set. Darling, you'll have such a good time. I doubt you'll get in any swimming, though it's possible the temperatures will be high enough for it. But you can swim any time, and there are far more exciting things to do there."

"I'm sure there are."

"So we have that to look forward to. Get a good night's sleep and I'll see you in the morning."

"Good night, then."

"Sleep well."

In bed Iris lay quiet and sick at heart.

To be involved in these machinations between Louisa and Paul Chandon was so distasteful to her that she felt physically ill. And that her aunt was so blindly infatuated that she would countenance such a thing was unbelievable.

Louisa, after all, planned to spend some months in Europe. Couldn't she have had the decency to postpone her affair until after her niece had left?

She was afraid of losing him, of course. She was afraid he'd lose interest.

There was one other explanation for Louisa's behavior, Iris thought, her heart pounding. If her affections for Paul Chandon were so strong, might she not consider *more* than an affair?

There were something like fourteen or fifteen years difference in age between Paul and Louisa. Things like that *could* happen… and sometimes did.

She sat up in bed. No, she thought fiercely. Oh no. Not Louisa. Not *her* aunt. The older wife of a money-hungry man who would bleed her, and bleed her.

There has got to be a way out of all this, Iris decided. She would just have to think of something.

And maddeningly, exhaustingly, all she could think of was that song on the Butte.

> *Toujours je t'aime chérie*
>
> *Always, my love, forever…*

And then the next three lines. The first half of the song.

Beyond that, the words refused to come to her.

Quit trying, she exhorted herself. For heaven's sake, there were *important* things to think about.

But the melody ran through her mind persistently, until she felt she would go mad.

If only they hadn't met Paul Chandon…and if only she hadn't heard that damned *song*…

Yet even in her dreams, when she finally fell asleep, the song was there, somewhere there, in her troubled mind.

Fourteen

Next morning, after a fitful night of tossing and turning, Iris was greeted by a knock at her door. "May I come in?" her aunt called.

"Please do."

"Will you forgive me, dear? I called my friend Kitty Sievers and they want me to breakfast with them at the Crillon, where they're staying. Do you mind?"

"No, of course not."

Louisa hesitated. "Darling, is it all right if I spend most of the day with them?"

"Certainly. I told you last night that it would be perfectly all right with me. I'm not a child, after all…a child you have to—"

Her aunt sat down on the edge of the bed. "Is anything the matter?" she asked.

Everything's the matter, Iris thought bleakly, but forced her face into a reassuring smile.

"Of course not. I just meant…oh, please do have a nice day with your friends. You know very well I'll find a hundred exciting things to do, particularly since it's my last day here."

"Not really, darling. I've decided to definitely bring you back here to Paris for a whole week after Nice. You can go to the Provence another time."

"That would be lovely."

Her aunt looked dissatisfied. "You seem a bit flushed to me." She put a hand on Iris's forehead. "Sure you're feeling all right?"

"Great. Super. Now run along."

"I've ordered breakfast for you. It will be up shortly."

"Thank you. Have fun."

"And we'll have a scrumptious dinner somewhere really good tonight. The Tour d'Argent, how's that?"

She got up. "And now I must run. Take care, darling."

"You too."

At last, Iris thought, when she was alone. At last she could put her mind to making order out of chaos. She had all morning and all afternoon to put on her thinking cap, dream up *some* way to avert a coming catastrophe. She simply could not *imagine* going through with this planned rendezous of her aunt's.

ROMANCE ON THE RIVIERA.

That her aunt, the proper Mrs. Henry Collinge, could scheme in such a Machiavellian manner…

And no suite at the hotel in Nice, Iris thought, fuming. Oh, no. Two singles and bath.

How *could* she!

What, oh what, could be done to prevent it?

A knock on the outside door heralded her breakfast which, when Matthieu brought it in and then left, Iris swallowed hastily, and then shoved the tray aside. The food tasted like straw.

She bathed and dressed, made up her face and brushed her hair, scarcely knowing what she was doing.

And then she was ready to go out, but stood in the middle of the room, frantic with indecision.

She had to *do* something…but what? To whom could she turn for help?

I should have had it out with Aunt Louisa, she thought. I should have told her I knew. Told her that I wouldn't be a party to her shenanigans.

That's what she should have done.

She could still do it. She could call the Crillon. Maybe her aunt and those friends of hers were still there, dawdling over breakfast in the dining room, yakking away.

She went over to the phone, picked up the receiver.

The operator said, *"Oui?"*

"Yes, please. I…I…"

I can't do it, Iris thought, sagging. She simply couldn't do it. She wouldn't know what to say or how to say it. She couldn't do it.

"Nothing," she said quickly into the receiver. *"Rien, merci,"* and then hung up the receiver with a little bang.

Her hands were shaking so that her tote bag, on the bedside table, slid off, and the contents spilled out onto the floor.

"Damn it," she said, and started scooping up tissues, wallet, postcards, map, card case…

It was then that something clicked in her mind.

The card case.

That man at the Place de l'Aima. Monsieur…

She sat down on the floor and fished out the card he had given her.

Monsieur Marchand, that was it. That nice man. That nice, older man.

"If you should ever be in trouble, or need a friend…"

He had been so kind, so sympathetic, she remembered. He had been the kind of person you felt you'd known all your life.

She thought about it. Thought about it for quite a while. After all, he was a stranger. She had talked to him for no more than a half hour. He would have forgotten her very existence by now.

You couldn't just call a perfect stranger, that you had exchanged a few words with for about half an hour and say, "I need help badly, please come to my rescue."

He'd think she was crazy.

And anyway, how could he possibly help her? What would be her purpose in contacting him? What could he do for her?

An odd little feeling came over her. A new, and rather startling feeling. It was a weird, almost frightening sensation. It was like seeing herself from the outside, as if part of her was looking down at herself, looking with a stranger's eyes…and eyes that were pitying…but at the same time critical.

As if this stranger were watching her as she sat on the floor of her Hotel Vendôme bedroom, brooding, uncertain, and forlorn.

She was suddenly conscious of her ridiculous sprawl on the floor, her whirling, unproductive thoughts, her juvenile approach to what was a very real problem.

For heaven's sake, she thought, springing up. She was twenty-four years old, a great gawk of a young woman who was behaving like a child of ten.

There came a time when Mommy and Daddy couldn't fix things for you, she told herself coldly. It was high time she faced that fact. It was high time she started acting her age.

Now, she thought, she had this man's card. He was not St. George, to fight a dragon for her. But he could, very likely, be of some use.

She thought it all out very carefully, step by step.

One: It was too late now to call her aunt at the Crillon.

Two: To confront her aunt with her knowledge of what was going on was something she couldn't, really and truly couldn't, bring herself to do.

Three: Therefore, she would telephone Monsieur Marchand. And assuming that she could reach him, what was she going to ask of him?

She finally decided that, since Monsieur Marchand was a native Parisian and an experienced, worldly gentleman, he might conceivably find out something about this Paul Chandon, something that would assure her aunt that to go any further with this liaison would be to her detriment and sorrow.

"That's it," she cried, triumphantly. That's what she would ask Claude Marchand to do.

She was no longer wringing her hands. She had made up her mind, like a mature person, and it only remained to telephone Claude Marchand.

When she went to the telephone this time there was no stupid hemming and hawing.

"Oui?" the operator's voice said.

"Will you call a number for me, please?"

"Certainly, Mademoiselle."

She gave him the number and waited.

It was ten to one, he would be out, Iris realized. But she waited calmly, and after about half a dozen rings, she heard a man's voice say, "Allo?"

"Hello," Iris said. "Am I speaking to Claude Marchand?"

"This is Claude Marchand."

The same heavy but velvety accent, the same charming intonations. Thank God he wasn't out somewhere, Iris thought, and took the plunge.

"You won't remember me, I'm afraid, but this is Iris Easton, and two days ago we met on the Place de l'Aima. You…my tote bag had fallen down and you—"

There was a low, pleased chuckle. "And I picked it up and woke you from a sound sleep," Claude Marchand said. "Hello, Mademoiselle Iris Easton. Are you still in love with Paris?"

"More so than ever," she replied, so grateful for his warmth and kindness that she could have cried. "Only I'm going to have to leave tomorrow. My aunt and I are bound for the Côte d'Azur."

"Very lovely at this time of year," he said approvingly. "You will enjoy it."

"There is a slight problem," she said quickly. "You were so kind, Monsieur, to say that if I should be in trouble I could call you." She swallowed. "This is a great imposition, I realize."

"Oh," he said, with a smile in his voice. "And I thought you were calling me because you had fallen in love with me and wanted to propose that we start an *amour.*"

She sat down on the bed and laughed softly. "What would you do," she asked him, "if I declared that I *would* like to start an *amour* with you?"

"I would faint," he said boomingly, "with delight."

Then he became serious. "What's the trouble, *chérie?*" he asked. "Is it about that young man who is causing you such distress?"

"Yes, it is," she said. "And I thought that…that somehow you might be able to…well, to find out something about him."

A fractional pause and then, "You mean his credentials," he said.

"More or less. You see, if his reputation is…if he's a notorious… if he makes a practice of preying on older women."

Another silence.

"That is," Iris finished, "do you think, if I gave you his name, you could ascertain whether he's one of those men who—"

"You mean you want me to find out if he's a cheap chiseler," Claude Marchand said, quite astonishing Iris with his knowledge of American lingo.

"Is that asking too much?" she asked humbly.

"Why, not at all," he replied. "What's this young scoundrel's name?"

"It's Paul Chandon. C-h-a-n-d-o-n."

This time there was a very long silence. So long that Iris was sure the connection had been broken.

When it seemed that, indeed, they had been cut off, she cried, "Monsieur? Are you there?"

"*Oui,*" he said, and then, "I assume that this young man is most attractive?"

"You assume correctly," she answered. "Like…oh, Charles Boyer, when Charles Boyer was young and—"

"And irresistible to his female audience," the man said. "Did you see him in *Pepe le Moko?*"

"Yes, at the Museum of Modern Art, in New York," she said. "With Hedy Lamarr. Anyway, he's that sort of man, only far more striking even."

"About what age is this man who is clinging to your aunt?" he asked.

"I would say thirty-one or two. Thereabouts."

"Dark-haired?"

"Yes, dark-haired. Dark eyes too. Very tanned. Expensive clothes."

"Ah?"

"And beautiful manners, except with me. He, naturally, dislikes me. I'm in the way, as you can understand."

"I wonder…" Claude Marchand said thoughtfully, and then fell silent again.

"Yes?" Iris demanded, twiddling her thumbs.

"Yes," he said. "I am thinking."

"Oh."

She waited again.

Then, "I wonder," he said musingly. "I really do wonder. Paul Chandon, yes? C-h-a-n-d-o-n?"

"Right."

"It strikes me a little funny," he said. "Paul Chandon. It's, of course, a very famous name here. Oh, I am sure there are many Chandons in Paris, and in France. It's not a name like Dupont, of course, which fills up about ten pages of the telephone book. But Chandon, when one thinks of it, inevitably means the wine family."

"The wine family?"

"*Bien sur.* Chandon, a household word. There is a Paul Chandon *père* and a Paul Chandon *fils*. Father and son. Theirs is one of the great distilleries of France. So naturally, when you speak of a Paul Chandon, one instantly thinks of *the* Paul Chandon."

"It couldn't be," Iris said flatly. "This young man doesn't do a bloody thing except hang around cafes."

"And make overtures to people like your aunt."

"Exactly. So how could it be *that* Paul Chandon?"

"But why not?" he argued. "Many younger men are partial to older women. Particularly when a certain young man lost his mother not very long ago. Perhaps he is lonely, and was in need of solace from a kind lady like your aunt."

This time it was Iris who was silent. The receiver had gone slack in her fingers. What *was* all this? Was he saying that there was a possibility of Paul Chandon's being Paul Chandon?

I mean, *the* Paul Chandon, she thought, sitting down quickly.

"Allo, allo," Monsieur Marchand said imperatively. "You are still there?"

"Yes."

"Well?"

Iris's lips were dry. "Is there any way I can find out if this man is…the wine family Paul Chandon?"

"Let me give it some thought," he said, and then suddenly, "Where are you now, Mademoiselle?"

"At my hotel."

"You told me where, but I have forgotten."

"Place Vendôme, the Hotel Vendôme."

"Ah yes, now I recall. What time is it? My clock is in another room."

Iris looked at her watch. "Almost eleven."

"Almost eleven. You are very near the Cafe de la Paix."

"Yes, I've been there and it's not far from here."

"Could you meet me there, say in half an hour?"

"Oh yes. You're quite sure it's not imposing?"

"I'm in the middle of a chapter," he told her. "But ask any writer. The slightest excuse will suffice to get one away from one's research difficulties and into the company of others."

"You're an author?"

"But don't think the less of me for it," he said, with a chuckle. "Otherwise I am perfectly normal."

"You're a…a wonderful person. Thank you, thank you. I'll dash right over to the Cafe de la Paix."

"*A tout à l'heure,*" he said cheerily, and rang off.

At the Cafe de la Paix, watching the passing parade on the street with unseeing eyes, Iris had a coffee, then another coffee and then, to soothe her frayed nerves, a cognac.

She had quite a long wait, but thirty-five minutes after she had sat down, a portly figure with a navy beret hove into sight. Monsieur Marchand had arrived.

"*Bonjour et félicitations,*" he said warmly, and plumped himself into a chair. "I am sorry, I was a bit delayed. The traffic in this city…Victor threatens every other day to leave me and go to work in some factory."

"Victor?" Iris asked, puzzled.

"My *chauffeur.* But he won't. Secretly, he likes the challenge." He smiled mellowly at Iris. "How nice to see you again, Mademoiselle Iris Easton."

"I seem to be taking a lot of advantage," she said ruefully. "But you see, what really upset me…upset me terribly, was that I found out, quite by accident, that this…this Paul Chandon is also going to the Riviera."

She flushed, and then added defiantly, "Well, I overheard a telephone call I wasn't supposed to and found that out. My aunt was very secretive about it. She didn't say anything to me, not one single thing. And the phone conversation sounded very… very equivocal, very…"

"Like a tryst?" he suggested.

She nodded, still flushing.

"And I didn't want her to be hurt…or victimized. You can understand that!"

"Yes, of course," he said soothingly. "You didn't want her to fall into the hands of a rogue."

He leaned toward her. "The question now is, however, whether or not you have been making a mistake about this young man, about any possible questionable intentions on his part."

She nodded wretchedly. "I guess that's about it."

"Well, I think we can find out without too much difficulty."

"You do?"

"Yes. I will ring up the Paris office of Paul Chandon et Cie and say that I understand M. Chandon the younger is bound for the Côte d'Azur in the next few days. I will pretend to be a journalist, say that I myself will be on the Côte d'Azur and that I wish to interview him for an article."

He beamed at her. "If the answer is yes, then we will indeed be certain that *your* Paul Chandon is the Paul Chandon I spoke of. The interview will be politely and regretfully denied, of course, as the Chandon family keeps—as you Americans say—a low profile. Personal publicity is something they are inclined to shun. However, it is an identity we are trying to establish, and the article is only a subterfuge."

A waiter approached, and Monsieur Marchand ordered a cognac for Iris and himself.

Then he regarded her speculatively.

"Suppose," he said, "that we find out that the young man in question is *my* Paul Chandon. What would your reaction be to that bit of news, Mademoiselle?"

Iris's fingers twisted in her lap. "I wouldn't know what to think," she said. "Monsieur Marchand…these Chandons you speak of. I suppose they're well off?"

"If I had their means," he said dryly, "I would spend the rest of my life doing nothing but enjoying life's pleasures. I would throw my typewriter away and sleep until noon every day." He smiled. "Of course I would do no such thing, any more than Victor would give up driving for me and go into a factory. But yes, *ma chére,* they are very well off indeed. Neither father nor son would have any reason to pursue an impressionable American woman for reasons of bettering their lot in life."

"I see."

"Ah, here are our drinks." He took a quick sip of the liqueur and then got up.

"And now I will make the call," he announced.

"You're sure you don't mind doing this?" Iris asked him.

"Why should I? This is a small adventure for me. It is all, as you ebullient Americans say, great fun."

He gave her a conspiratorial wink and then, expertly weaving his way through the nests of tables and chairs, went inside the cafe.

Iris waited, trying not to think, which was like saying, trying not to breathe, because the whole thing was beginning to assume the proportions of a nightmare.

She needed a good, stiff drink. Not cognac, but a good old honest martini.

Claude Marchand was gone for a very long time. I'll go nuts, Iris thought, crossing and uncrossing her legs.

At last he came back. Tense, on edge, Iris watched his progress throught the clutter of tables. Once someone tapped him on the arm, and Iris saw his eyes light up. He even sat down briefly, and spoke a few animated words to a man of about his own age.

Then he got up and made his way back to her.

He picked up what was left of his cognac and tossed it off. "I made two telephone calls," he told her. "I couldn't get any information whatsoever from the office of the Chandon firm, so I had to fall back on a friend who works on a newspaper."

"Did you find out anything?" Iris asked him anxiously.

"I did. My newspaper friend made one phone call and found out two important things. He rang up a service that provides information about people of newsworthy interest. Every newspaper, magazine and film company uses this celebrity service.

In short, Mademoiselle, Paul Chandon *fils* has booked a flight to Nice leaving Paris on Wednesday."

He lifted his shoulders expressively. "I think," he said, "that we can be quite certain that the young man you know is the same Paul Chandon."

"I can't believe it," Iris whispered. The sun, mercilessly bright, blinded her. She was conscious of Claude Marchand's eyes on her, of his curious, blue-eyed scrutiny.

"I just don't know what it means," she said finally.

"Why don't you drink that cognac," he suggested. "You look a bit pale."

"I'd like a martini. Could I have a martini?"

"You won't get a decent martini here," he told her. "How about scotch?"

"Yes, all right."

He signalled for the waiter. "Johnnie Walker, no ice, no water." He snapped his fingers. "*Tout de suite*. The young lady is feeling ill."

"*Oui oui.*"

The scotch was brought on the double.

"Drink it," M. Marchand ordered.

Obediently, Iris raised the glass to her lips.

"All down, finish it," he said authoritatively.

She swallowed the rest of it and felt its effects almost immediately.

"Better?" her friend asked.

"Yes, thank you."

"And now," M. Marchand said, "would you like to know what I think this is all about, this business of your aunt and Paul Chandon?" He gave her a quick, somewhat defensive look. "Remember," he reminded her, "that I am a writer, with an imagination that sometimes runs away with me. Yet, if I were not, I might be just as puzzled as you are yourself."

"Please go on," she implored him.

"Very well. We are, after my friend's telephone calls, 99 and 99/100ths percent certain that the young man who has caused you such anguish and the son of the Chandon dynasty are one and the same. Yes?"

"I guess so."

"Now, you claim that he persistently clings to your aunt, which has been a great worry, since you have suspected that he has eyes for her money. Yes?"

"Yes."

"Only, since the Chandon family is fortunate enough to have amassed a considerable fortune, this would not make sense." He searched her face. "Would it?" he persisted.

"No."

"Then what is he after?"

"I don't know," she muttered.

There was such a long silence that she raised her eyes and, though the shade of her sunglasses, saw a faint smile on his face.

"Do you know?" she asked.

"I don't know," he said softly. "But I can conjecture."

"I'd be very grateful if you'd tell me," she said faintly.

"I will, but I think you have already started to guess. You are a bright, intelligent, aware young lady. So I doubt it will be too difficult for you to reach the same conclusions I have. In other words, Mademoiselle, I feel very strongly that this Paul Chandon, whom we both probably agree is the Paul Chandon of the distilleries, is in fact someone your aunt knows well—he, and his family. And that for some reason I personally can not surmise, your aunt wanted you to meet him as a stranger." He looked keenly at her. "Could that be impossible," he asked.

"Why, I met him purely by accident," Iris cried. "We were at this small cafe on the Place St. Michel, and he pretended I'd lost something from my bag. It wasn't true…he simply took it out of my bag and…"

The scene came back to her. First the walk up the Quai des Grands Augustins, then the bookstalls. And in a replay of the morning of their second day, something else. Her aunt tugging at her arm, as she looked at her watch, and saying something like, "We've spent enough time here, Iris…"

And then, as they were sitting in the cafe, Louisa had again looked at her watch.

More than that! The phone call, that first evening, which Louisa had simply said, casually, had been from a friend. A call that could have led to an arranged meeting.

But he had picked her pocket!

"Why should she do it like that?" she cried passionately. "If she wanted to introduce me to someone…a man…"

M. Marchand's eyes were curious and attentive.

There was another flashback. This time in Manhattan. Her aunt saying, "Oh, and I know young men who can take you to discos and the theater…"

And herself: "Auntie, you won't try to matchmake?"

"Have you come up with any answers?" M. Marchand asked.

"Possibly. If you don't mind, may I have another scotch?"

"Just one more, because I think you need it."

When it was in front of her, she took a deep swallow.

"Oh yes. Thank you." She leaned on the table and shook her head. "Yes, I guess I do have some ideas about the whole thing," she said slowly. "I think that, with the best intentions in the world, my aunt tried to play God with my life. She shouldn't have done it."

She raised brimming eyes, choked, and looked down again.

"You think your aunt arranged something," M. Marchand said. "Yes, I too feel that it must have been along those lines. I don't know why she did it, but—" He put a thoughtful finger to his lips. "But she must have had her reasons," he said finally. "And it's not anything to be unhappy about, is it? You were worried about your aunt and there is no longer any reason to worry. There is left only the fact that, as I see it, this young man has fallen in love with you, was attracted at first meeting, and what was originally planned to be just a man and a girl enjoying a few good times together became something else. Something so powerful, in fact, that he chooses to join you on the Côte d'Azur."

M. Marchand leaned back in his chair. "You have made a conquest, Mademoiselle." he said softly. "No man goes rushing after a girl the way young Paul is doing…unless he is badly smitten."

He shook his head regretfully. "A pity you don't care for him," he commented. "Too bad you dislike him so much."

"How could I like him when I thought he was an unsavory character?" she cried.

"True," he said. "I don't like unsavory characters either."

"*That* was the reason I disliked him."

"But you don't dislike him otherwise?"

She slumped in her chair. What was the use? What in the world was the use of fighting it? Dislike Paul? Why, even when she had thought he was an unpleasant, grasping type she had been drawn to him, had responded to his wonderful good looks, his magnetism, his voice, his manner, his body contact.

"No," she said breathlessly. "I don't dislike him otherwise. In fact, even when I thought he was up to no good, I…I wanted to like him. I was attracted, but…well, my defenses have been up for quite a long time. I resisted any involvement that might hurt me. That might hurt me *again*."

She twisted her fingers miserably. "I was so rude to him," she said. "Rude and horrid. I feel awful."

"But still he stuck around, and is now going to follow you somewhere else, so his feelings for you must be very strong. But

I wouldn't worry, Mademoiselle. You can make it up to him. On the Riviera, there will be blue skies, warm and sunny days, and long, romantic evenings."

M. Marchand drained the last of his cognac and gave her a sly little look. "As a matter of fact," he told her, "you might be able to straighten this out today."

"How?" she demanded. "We're leaving tomorrow and how could I do anything today?"

"My friend's call to our celebrity service netted him some additional information," he said. "It seems that Paul Chandon, on almost every afternoon at around five o'clock, takes his aperitif at *Le Moineau,* on the Rue Vernet. So it is very possible that he would be there *this* afternoon."

He folded his arms. "If, as it seems likely, he will be there, then of course you will be certain that there has been no mistake…that the Paul you know is the Paul Chandon I have been talking about. And after that, you can, as you say, straighten things out."

He smiled hearteningly at her. "Is your stomach tied up in knots, Mademoiselle?"

"Yes," she admitted.

"Then you are probably in love. That's nice. I envy you."

"But aren't you married?"

"My dear wife died four…no, five years ago. But I have a daughter and a son-in-law and two grandchildren. And a mistress."

"Oh, I see."

He chuckled. "My writing," he said, "is my mistress. And a most demanding one."

"And I mustn't keep you any longer! Thank you. *Thank* you. You've been so kind to me. I'm more grateful than I'd ever be able to say."

"Don't lose my card," he said. "I would be happy to know the outcome of this little story. So I hope that I will hear from you again."

He glanced at the bill the waiter gave him, pulled some money out of his pocket and, taking Iris's arm, walked out to the sidewalk with her.

He picked up her hand and kissed it gently. "The Rue Vernet is just off the Etoile," he said. "Not hard to find."

He smiled his blue-eyed smile and bowed. *"Bonne chance,"* he said warmly. "Good luck, Iris Easton."

She watched him go off, spry, jaunty and with a springing step. I owe that man a great deal, she thought. Some day I hope I can repay his kindness.

Then she looked at her watch. It was just one o'clock. At five o'clock, on almost every afternoon, Paul Chandon had an aperitif at *Le Moineau,* on the Rue Vernet, just off the Etoile.

There were hours to kill.

Easy enough, in Paris, to while away hours. It was just that five o'clock seemed so very far away. And time had suddenly become very precious.

Fifteen

Iris approached the cafe *Le Moineau* at a few minutes before five.

It was a modest building, but it had a large, cheerful outside area with a picture of a sparrow on its sheltering canopy.

It was the second time that day she had seen it. An hour earlier she had canvassed the territory off the Etoile, in order to find the cafe and be sure she knew where it was.

An hour earlier there had been only a sprinkling of patrons. Now, however, the place was jumping, with most of the tables occupied and a lot of noise and laughter as Parisians, stopping by for their after-work drink before going home to supper, talked over the events of the day with friends and colleagues.

Iris stood a slight distance away and tried to breathe normally. She was tired from walking about, apprehensive, shivery and terribly afraid that, after all, Paul would think she was insane to hunt him down like this.

What if his feelings for her were only minimal? What if everything that had seemed so logical while she was talking to M. Marchand wasn't *like* that?

She stood, irresolute and suddenly dejected, near a boxwood hedge that made a place of concealment for her. What am I doing? she asked herself agitatedly.

Supposing that the Paul Chandon who took his afternoon aperitif at this cafe was not *her* Paul Chandon? In that case the other Paul Chandon would be unknown to her…and there would be no one she recognized here.

Her thoughts became so muddled that she felt a wave of vertigo, and a terrible feeling of loneliness.

It suddenly occurred to her that whichever Paul Chandon was going to come for an aperitif would probably come from the direction of the Etoile. Horrified at the possibility of being seen before she wanted to be, she left her place of shelter and walked swiftly to the farther end of the cafe. The hedge, on this side too, was a small haven from which she could resume her watch.

And then, as her heart jumped sickeningly in her chest, she saw him.

It was Paul. It was Paul...*her* Paul!

So it's true, she thought dizzily. M. Marchand had guessed right. This was the Paul Chandon of the wine family.

She stared, transfixed. Paul, tall, erect, his steps jaunty and casually assured, gave a glance around, and then chose a table that was more or less centrally situated. He pulled out a chair, sat down in it and, without even looking round, raised a hand for a waiter.

In a second or two a *garçon* was at his side. Iris could hear the interchange clearly.

"Dubonnet blonde," Paul said and then, looking up, added, *"Ca va, Francois?"*

"Bien, et vous?"

"Comme ci, comme çà."

The waiter went away, and when he came back it was with the drink and a newspaper. There was a nod from Paul, and the waiter went off.

Still Iris hesitated. He could be waiting for someone...say, a pretty, chic young French girl, with sexy eyes and a Parisian dash.

I have to be sure, Iris thought.

She saw Paul take a sip of his drink and then open the newspaper. But he could be waiting for someone...

She regarded him from her stance at the boxwood hedge. There he was, *her* Paul Chandon, the man who had stirred her heart after many a long hiatus. For almost two years Iris Easton had told herself that falling in love was dangerous...falling in love could break your heart.

But that was long ago and far away, she told herself now, as she gazed at the man who had dashed down the barriers and let love in again.

Paul, she thought. Oh, Paul, my dearest love.

Yet she was wary and, she told herself, better to be safe than sorry. It was all or nothing now, so far as she was concerned and she had to be sure that *her* Paul was not expecting a young female companion.

She turned away and fixed her eyes on her watch. Five minutes more, she decided. I'll give it five minutes more.

Please God, let him be alone when I look again, she prayed, as the minutes ticked off, and when at last she did let her eyes dart back to his table he was still alone and reading his newspaper, absorbed in its contents.

It was now almost five-twenty.

He's not waiting for anyone, Iris decided jubilantly. He was going to be alone, she was sure of it. She watched him light a cigarette, and thought, he's so wonderful to look at.

It was now or never, she told herself, and walked toward him.

He didn't see her until she stood at his table. Then, sensing a presence, he looked up—looked up and stared incredulously at her.

"Hello, Paul," Iris said.

He kept staring at her.

"I just happened to be passing by," she said, and to her amazement her voice was strong and clear. "And I saw you sitting here."

He kept on looking at her in that stunned, befuddled way before he jumped up, spilling his drink and knocking the newspaper off the table.

"Oh, I *am* sorry," Iris cried, and knocked heads with him as both made an attempt to retrieve the paper. At the same time a sticky liquid, from the spilled drink, trickled down her neck.

"*Mon Dieu,*" Paul muttered, swiping at her with a handkerchief he pulled out of his pocket. "I am so sorry."

"No, my fault," Iris protested.

A boy came over with a rag and cleaned off the table top with a philosophical shrug, then left, the sopping cloth held gingerly in his hand.

"Is your dress spoiled?" Paul asked anxiously.

"No, it's wash and wear, don't give it another thought."

"But sit down, please!"

She slid into a chair.

"It was just such a surprise to see you," Paul said, sitting down too.

He looked warily at her, warily and questioningly, and suddenly he seemed very young, even, in an odd way, younger than herself. He sat on the edge of his chair, and the assured man she had watched from her vantage point at the edge of the cafe, became someone else…someone not certain of his ground.

"Paul, are you waiting for someone?" Iris asked quietly.

"Waiting for someone?"

"I mean…a girl, a companion?"

"No," he said. "I come here alone…nearly every afternoon. For my aperitif…and then I go home. I am not waiting for anyone."

"All right, then," she said, and it was not so difficult after all. "It's not true, Paul, that I just happened to be passing by. I came here because I was told you might be here. I'm glad you are, because there's something I want to say to you."

She quickly put on her sunglasses. It was because of the late afternoon sun, and the dazzlement of his dark eyes looking into hers…and his nearness.

"Paul," Iris went on, "I found out a few things quite by chance. Never mind how. But I did. And I just want you to know that I had an entirely wrong idea of you, and I know I was hateful. So

I came here to apologize. Whatever I said, whatever I did, please forgive me."

She looked away, swallowing, and then back at him. "The masquerade is over, Paul. I know who you are. And I know that you and my aunt are friends. I know that she must be well acquainted with your family. But I forgive you both for setting up this little charade. The main thing is, I want you to understand why I was so unpleasant to you."

"Wait," he said, holding up a hand. "Wait, Iris. Your aunt is not an acquaintance of my family. Nor of mine. Ah yes, she is a friend of mine *now*, and I think she is a charming and lovely lady. But before a week ago I had never seen her in my life. Not until that day when I met you both in the Place St. Michel."

"I don't understand," Iris said, pushing her sunglasses up to her forehead.

"Nor do I, Iris. All I know is that I saw you at that cafe and I told myself that I wanted to meet this girl and get to know her. Why? I asked myself. Why was it so important to know this girl? Of all the girls one sees, that one girl stands out and…"

He seemed almost angry. "You were just a pretty girl," he said, gesturing. "A young…really *too* young American girl like those one sees in Paris every summer, every year. And you were not very receptive. In fact, you were decidedly hostile. Perhaps that was it…that I wanted to put you in your place. It was a challenge."

She nodded. "I know I was unfriendly and…and hostile, as you said. You picked my pocket, admit it! Pretended that something had fallen out of it. So I was peeved about that, and then later I thought you were after my aunt for her money."

The impact suddenly jolted her. "You don't really mean to say that my aunt is a stranger to you?" she demanded.

"She was then," he said emphatically.

"And all this wasn't planned?"

"I certainly didn't plan to fall in love with you," he said loudly, so loudly that heads were turned in their direction.

He glared at the amused glances that came their way, and lowered his voice. "Which, to my concern and discomfort, I did," he finished and lit a cigarette with fingers that shook slightly.

"I didn't plan to fall in love with you either, but apparently I did," Iris said bravely.

The waiter came over, pencil poised over his pad. "*Oui*, Mademoiselle?" he said to Iris.

"Later," Paul said irritably. "Go away, Francois."

"Oh la la," the man said, walking off with a grin.

"Say it again, what you just said," Paul demanded. "I want to be sure I heard you correctly. Say it again."

"I didn't plan to fall in love with you," Iris repeated, her face on fire.

"You didn't plan to…but you did? You said you did?"

"Somewhere along the way," she muttered, looking at her fingernails.

"And you do now? You're…you care for me?"

"Why are you so surprised?" she cried. "You're an attractive man…you must know that!"

"You are a beautiful girl, but that doesn't mean that every man in the world falls in love with you."

"True," she said, her eyes focused on the box hedges that bordered the cafe.

There was a little pause and then Paul said, "Don't look over there. Look at me, Iris."

"I'm looking at you," she said, and dragged her eyes away from the shrubbery.

"Why, *chérie*," Paul said, searching her face. "Am I to believe that you mean what you say? That you say? That you…that you do care for me?"

She pulled her sunglasses down again.

"I told you I did…do," she said. "What more can I say?"

"Much more," he replied. "But for the moment, it's enough. Iris, my dear, my sweet…ah, Iris…"

He threw back his head and breathed deeply of the perfumed Paris air. He laughed jubilantly, and slapped a hand on the table.

"Iris Easton, I love you," he said ringingly, and once more heads were turned on them from surrounding tables.

Paul, swiveling in his chair, gave everyone in sight a benign and cordial bow. "You see, I love her," he announced. "What do you think of that?"

There was a general clapping of hands, while Iris wanted to fall through the floor. A chorus of good-natured laughter rippled through the seated throng.

"Everybody knows it now," Paul said, turning back to her. "Don't be embarrassed. The French have a great respect for love."

His dark eyes plumbed her own. "And so it seems, *chérie*, that we have found each other. What came before is of no import. There is only the future to consider."

"Yes, the future," she echoed, trembling.

"Together?"

"Are you sure you mean that?" she asked shakily.

"I mean for as long as we both shall live," he said. "I mean forever. Say yes, please, and then I will tell you what we are going to do with our first evening alone together. But first you must say it. Is it yes, Iris?"

"Yes," she answered. And then said it again. "Yes. Oh, yes, Paul."

"*C'est si bon!*" he cried exuberantly. "When your aunt learns about this! She will be surprised…not about me, naturally…she knows very well my feelings for you. She has been my *confidante*. And at one point I admit I was ready to give up. That was in the beginning, and I told myself it would be useless…that you were cold and…and even narcissistic, and I want, and *need* warmth and love, *chérie*…to give it, and receive it. But then I couldn't give up."

He smiled at her. "We French have a saying. *'C'est plus fort pour moi.'* It was too strong for me."

"Obviously it was too strong for me too," Iris commented. "Not that I didn't fight it. But then, of course, I was convinced you were a snake in the grass. After my aunt, for her money. So you see, it's all due to Claude Marchand that—"

"To whom?"

"Claude Marchand. A man I met one afternoon on the Place de l'Alma. An *older* man, Paul, and it's just occurred to me that he might be free for dinner tonight. That is, if I ring him up right away."

She shushed Paul as he prepared to put in a few objections. "Yes, I too would like it to be just the two of us tonight," she said. "But I do feel we owe it to Aunt Louisa to have her with us. I've been thinking such dreadful things about her. So, Paul, wouldn't it be nice if the four of us could be together? I owe so much to M. Marchand, and he's a widower and seems a little lonely…"

"And your aunt is a widow, and perhaps a little lonely?" he suggested.

"I was only thinking of a casual, pleasant friendship between them," she protested.

"I read you," he said, "like a book. You are thinking of much more than that. But go call him and we will all four dine together. It's a lot to give up, not to have you alone tonight, but to please you, *chérie,* I would do almost anything."

"Thank you," Iris said, getting up. She bent and put her lips to his forehead. "I'll be right back, *chéri.*"

Marveling at how naturally the French endearment had come to her, she found her way into the interior of the cafe, located a small and stuffy phone booth, squeezed herself into it, and once more spoke to Claude Marchand.

"Ah," he said, when she announced herself. "I was wondering how soon I would hear from you. You sound very blithe, so perhaps everything is all right?"

"Everything is so all right I could do an Irish jig," she told him. "Would you by any chance be free for dinner this evening? With me, my aunt, and Paul Chandon…your Paul Chandon and mine. Oh, I hope you're free to come with us!"

"How delightful. I had planned to work until around ten and then fry myself some chicken livers. Once again you have saved me from hours of arduous toil, Mademoiselle. Yes, I am free for dinner, thank you very much."

"Could you possibly meet us at our hotel, Monsieur?" She looked at her watch. "Say, at around seven?"

"I will be happy to. Unfortunately, I keep forgetting *what* hotel you are staying at."

"The Hotel Vendôme, on the Place Vendôme."

"Ah yes, Then, until seven o'clock. *A bientôt,* Iris Easton."

She was very pleased with herself when she hung up. Dialing the number of the hotel, she had a vision of Aunt Louisa and Claude Marchand walking off into the sunset together. "Allo?" the operator's voice said.

"Yes, Mrs. Collinge's room, please."

There were three rings and then the voice of her aunt came to her, sounding a bit cranky.

"It's me, Iris."

"Iris Easton, where *are* you? It's after six and you're not even here! Where *are* you?"

"On my way back to the hotel. I'll be there in ten minutes. Fifteen at the most."

"I've been frantic! I very nearly called the gendarmes!"

"What could happen to me. I'm perfectly all right. I'm with Paul and all four of us are going to have dinner together."

"All four of whom? What do you mean you're with Paul?"

"It's a long story," Iris said. "I have to go now, but I'll see you shortly."

"Iris. Iris!"

"I love you, Aunt Louisa," Iris said softly, and hung up.

When she went outside again, Paul had apparently paid the check and was standing, looking at his watch and tapping his newspaper impatiently on the table top.

"I had to make two calls," Iris explained. "My aunt was a bit worried about me, so I must hurry home. And yes, Claude Marchand is having dinner with us tonight. Would you get me a cab, please, and I'll dash back and change."

"I'll go with you," he said authoritatively. "I'll wait in the bar until you and your aunt are ready."

They were walking up the Rue Vernet and, as they neared the corner Paul, in plain sight of half a dozen passersby, put both arms around her and pulled her up against himself.

"But first," he said huskily, "this. Our first kiss. No, don't fight me, sweetheart. What does it matter if people are looking? What does anything matter?"

What *did* it matter, she thought, clinging to him. His lips, gentle at first and then hungry and demanding, engaged her own. Who cared if a few jaded Parisians were eyeing them curiously? It was, as Paul said, their first kiss and, Iris thought tremulously, she would remember it, and this magical moment, forever.

Then he released her and, as they walked ahead to find a taxi at the Etoile, told her what his plans for the evening were.

"We will go up to the Place du Tertre again," he said. "And after dinner walk down the steps as we did the other night. There are eight…perhaps nine flights of them, and on each one I will kiss you. It means that, by the time we reach the bottom, I will have kissed you about one hundred and ninety times."

He grinned down at her. "How is that for a start, Mademoiselle?"

"I'm looking forward to it, Monsieur," she replied.

Paris, Iris thought, was wonderful, simply wonderful. You met the nicest people.

"And, oh yes," Paul said suddenly. "I will have the violinist play our song again, during which we will hold each other's hands and look into each other's eyes. This time it will mean even more."

His arm was slung over her shoulder, the way Iris had seen the young boy hold his girl in the student quarter on the day she and Paul had met.

It was liking, she thought, as well as loving. Being comrades as well as lovers.

A passionate kiss…and then an arm slung over her shoulder.

And because her heart was at last ready to accept them, the last lines of "their" song came to Iris effortlessly and without thought, as if the words had flowed from Paul's mind to her own.

> *Mine is a heart sincere*
> *My passion for you shall never*
> *Ever lose its madness*
> *Never until I die.*

Sixteen

After leaving Paul in the bar lounge on the second floor, Iris ran up the next two flights of stairs. Before she had a chance to turn the key in the lock, the door was smartly opened by Louisa, a very confused Louisa.

"What happened?" she demanded. "You said you were with Paul. How? What's happened? Paul? You said you were with Paul? How in the world…"

"Give me a chance to catch my breath," Iris pleaded.

"Why did you hang *up* on me? Without telling me—"

"Take it easy, Auntie. To use one of my mother's pet phrases, everything's turned out all right. And I apologize, profusely, for thinking those horrible things about you."

"What horrible things? Iris, will you please try to make some sense?"

"I did think awful things," Iris admitted. "I've been thinking all along that you were madly infatuated with Paul. Yes, that's what I thought. And I was convinced that Paul was a cad and a bounder and was scheming to get you in his clutches and then squander your money right and left—besides making a fool of you. You can understand that I couldn't sit meekly by and see *that* happen. Not to you, Aunt Louisa. Oh, not to you."

"You thought that…you thought…

Louisa groped for a chair and sat down fast. "You actually thought that I would…and Henry dead only…"

"Other women have—"

"I'm not other women!" Louisa said shrilly. "You actually thought I'd lost my head over that *boy?*"

"He's not a boy," Iris said, her own voice rising. "He's a man…a wonderful, mature, tender, dear, wonderful, wonderful *man!*"

She threw out her arms dramatically. "So why shouldn't you lose your head over him?"

"But I didn't! How could you even think such a thing? And what made you think it?"

"Because you were always talking secretively together, and with my own eyes I saw you both holding hands in the bar the night we went to Montmartre. Oh, I know *now* that he was confiding in you, and—"

"He talked my ear off," Louisa cried. "About did I think there was a chance for him…and then you seemed to soften up quite a bit at *Mère Catherine's* on the Butte. So I thought, and so did he, that perhaps on the Riviera, which is certainly a spot where even the most resistant women are prone to be pushovers for romance, you might very well capitulate. So he booked a flight for the day after our own, and…"

"Yes, I know. I know everything."

"Then will you kindly explain *how* you know, and how you happened to be with him when you phoned me. I am struggling for composure, Iris, and if you don't tell me at once *from the beginning*, I shall explode."

"Please don't explode. M. Marchand will be here at seven, and it's after six-thirty now."

She ran a hand through her hair, "And I have to bathe and dress in less than half an hour!"

"M. Marchand?" Louisa looked absolutely bewildered.

"The man who put me on the right track. He's having dinner with us. Paul and I and you and M. Marchand. It's a celebration."

"A celebration?"

"Oh, please don't repeat everything I say! Look at the time!"

"What kind of a celebration?"

"Like an engagement party. For Paul and me."

"*Engagement* party?"

"Yes, and you might say you're happy for me."

"Iris…"

"Yes, it's true, Aunt Louisa. I'm going to marry him. For as long as we both shall live, he said."

Unaccountably she burst into tears.

"Iris…"

And then, just as suddenly, Louisa's eyes filmed over.

In the next moment they were in each other's arms until Iris pulled away. "I'm so happy I don't know what to do," she sobbed. "And look at the time!"

"Oh, Iris…"

"You're glad for me too, aren't you, Auntie?"

"Glad? I'm ecstatic! Dry your tears and sit right down and tell me from the start. I'm so at sea about the whole thing. Tell me everything."

"I will, but not now. I have to get dressed. He'll be here at seven, you see. But Paul's downstairs in the lounge, and when Claude Marchand arrives he can join Paul there."

"Who *is* this Claude Marchand?"

"I told you. He's the one who—"

She broke off. "Aunt Louisa, you simply must pull yourself together," she said firmly. "Because I'll never be ready by seven o'clock. You'll have to do the honors along with Paul. M. Marchand is a very fine gentleman and I know we'll have a perfectly super evening."

She gave her aunt an assessing look. Louisa, who was wearing one of her most beautiful dresses, in a heavenly shade of peacock blue, looked her very best. Her hair shone, her heart-shaped face was radiant with joy, curiosity and excitement, and her eyes were dewy with her recent tears.

"You look lovely," Iris said softly. "Perfectly lovely. Will you listen for the phone, which will probably ring in my room. It will be M. Marchand, so please ask him to go to the second floor lounge and ask for Paul's table."

She headed for her bedroom. "And now I simply must do something about myself," she said. "I'll hurry just as fast as I can, but I'm depending on you, Aunt Louisa, to keep Paul and M. Marchand company until I can join you."

"But Iris…"

"Just listen for my phone, okay?"

She left her aunt standing in the middle of the room with her mouth slightly open and in her shower heard the shrilling telephone, and then her aunt's voice.

As she was drying herself there was a knock at the bathroom door.

"Iris?"

"Yes?"

"He's here."

"M. Marchand?"

"Yes."

"Did you tell him to go to the—"

"I told him to go to the lounge and ask for Paul's table."

"Good girl. Now you go down too, and I promise I won't be long."

"No, I'll wait for you."

"You will not," Iris said, opening the door. She stood there wrapped in one of the enormous hotel towels. "I can't hurry if I'm not alone. And I do want to look decent tonight."

"You look pretty smashing as you are now."

"Ha ha. Hurry, now. It would be rude to keep him waiting. Oh, do go down and all of you have a drink. And let me get dressed!"

"A complete stranger," Louisa grumbled.

"He won't be for long. He talks a blue streak."

"Well, all right. But please, Iris, do hurry, won't you?"

"The sooner you go, the faster I can hurry."

At last she was by herself and free to slip into undies, hose, and then do something to her face. The tan helped, and there was really only a light lipstick and eye makeup to be applied. A quick brush of her hair and she was ready to put on her dress.

She didn't have to decide. She had one really good designer dress, for very special occasions. She slipped it over her head and stood looking at herself in the long pier glass.

"You are beautiful," he had said. *"Very beautiful."*

And tonight even Iris was able to concede that she would do. Pretty she had been born, and pretty she was, and thankful for it.

But beautiful?

If she was beautiful in Paul's eyes, then she was beautiful. It didn't matter what she thought…only what he did.

She quickly emptied the personal things from her tote bag and transferred them to a dressy one, then looked at the bag affectionately. That tote bag…that tote bag had introduced her to Paul Chandon, as it had introduced her to Claude Marchand. That idiotic tote bag had changed her life.

You dear thing, she said to it. I will never throw you away, never.

Then she let herself out, locked the door and walked quickly down the two flights of stairs and came almost face to face with Paul.

He was standing a few paces down the hall from the door of the lounge.

He put a quick finger to his lips and shook his head. Then he lifted a finger and beckoned to her.

She walked over to him cautiously. He was clearly indicating that she should be silent.

"What?" she whispered.

"Look inside," he whispered back.

From where they stood, she could see inside the room. There was Marcel at his bar, busy with bottles and glasses. Past the bar, a lot of people were sitting at the tables, and the room hummed with the sound of voices.

At one of the tables, and not very far away, sat Louisa and Claude Marchand.

Louisa, in her peacock-blue dress, a drink in front of her and a cigarette in her hand, was listening intently. M. Marchand, sans beret and clothed in a charcoal-gray suit with a discreet pin stripe, was a study in sartorial splendor. His thick hair, streaked with gray, was as neat as a schoolboy's.

He was speaking animatedly, with occasional expressive gestures of his hands—typically Gallic gestures—and was apparently relating some anecdote that seemed to fascinate his companion.

Whatever it was, the ending of it must have been amusing, because, as Iris watched, her aunt broke into delighted laughter.

"They appear to be enjoying each other's company," Paul said in a low voice and, putting a hand on Iris's arm, drew her farther down the hall.

"I made an excuse to leave for a few minutes," he told her. "They hit it off right away. Really, it was because Marchand has such an easy manner. He has a way of taking charge, hasn't he?"

"Do you like him?"

"Oh yes, very much indeed."

"So do I. And it looks as if my aunt does. Paul, it won't hurt for them to know each other. And then let come what may. Oh, I know you think I'm trying to—"

"Yes, I think you are trying to bring two people together. I am not critical, *chérie*. You are sweet. You want everyone to be happy."

"Because I'm happy."

"And so am I. Oh, am I! Anyway, I excused myself, saying there was a call I had to make. That would give them some time, I thought, to become friends, so that we would have a really enjoyable evening together."

"Aren't you nice."

"Am I?"

"Yes. I think you're wonderful."

"You do?"

"Unreservedly."

"Anyway," he said. "I did make a call. I tried to switch my flight to Nice for tomorrow, in order to be on your plane."

He made a long face, and shrugged.

"Oh. You couldn't do it. The flight was filled?"

"You are disappointed?"

"A little."

"Don't be," he said. "I was successful. I leave on the same flight as yours."

"Oh, Paul! I thought…"

"Just teasing," he said, and looked around quickly.

The corridor was empty, and he turned her so that her back was to the wall.

"Now," he said, "I have you in my power, Mademoiselle."

"I can always scream for help."

"I can always shut you up."

"How?" she started to say, but then his mouth came down on hers, and in a flash they were like one person, body to body, mouth to mouth, and whether it was his heart or her own Iris felt throbbing with such wild intensity, she couldn't have said if her life depended on it.

She knew only that never, at any moment of her life, had she imagined such joy and passion, such rapture and bliss…ecstasy that was almost like pain.

Whatever she had known of love…or thought she had known, paled into insignificance in the face of this overwhelming surge of exaltation…this transport of glory…this yearning, burning passion.

He let her go finally, and held her gently for a moment until both were able to speak again.

"Come, we must go," Iris said breathlessly. "They'll think we've been kidnapped."

"Yes, we must go," he agreed, settling his tie. "Anyway, we should conserve our energies. For those one hundred and ninety kisses on the steps down from the Butte."

"If they're anything like that one," she said, as they went into the lounge, "I'll end up in the hospital. I think you just broke three of my ribs."

"Well, there you are at last," Louisa said gaily, and a genial Claude Marchand stood up at their approach.

"*Bon soir,* Iris Easton," he said warmly.

"*Bon soir,* Claude Marchand."

"So I was wrong in my conjectures," he said, and shrugged. "But as you Americans say, you can't win them all."

"You were wrong, but you were right," she said. "Half right and half wrong."

"Yet it doesn't really matter, does it," he remarked. "As long as the ending came out all right."

"Forgive me for contradicting you, M. Marchand," Paul said. "But it is not the ending. It is only the beginning."

A Sneak Peek from Crimson Romance
(From *The Glass Orchid* by Emma Barron)

London, 1820

Rhys Camden swirled his brandy, watching the amber liquid coat the sides of the glass, slosh over the rim, and soak into the slightly worn carpet of the gambling club.

"I believe you are supposed to drink the brandy, Camden, not wash the floors with it. Though God knows Belford's could use a thorough cleaning."

Camden slowly brought his gaze up from his glass and tried to settle it on his friend, Drew Wittingham, but the man seemed intent on flittering around. Or perhaps it was just that Camden could no longer focus on anything after consuming so much brandy.

"Why *did* we decide to celebrate at Belford's," Wittingham continued, "instead of a more fashionable club? Surely Maven's would have been a more suitable place." Wittingham cast a red-rimmed eye around the club, a look of disdain etching his features as he took in the raucous crowd.

"Well, for one, we aren't members at Maven's."

"Ah, yes. I like to forget that we are not of the highest echelons of society. Pity, really, that even with all of your money you can't just buy yourself a title and be done with it."

"It isn't *my* money," Camden reminded his friend.

"Your money, your father's money." Wittingham dismissed the distinction with a wave of his hand. "It's all the same. Especially since you are now twenty-one and joining the family business."

"And that's the other reason we are at Belford's. Farber decided it was the most s-suitable place for the debauchery sure to occur at my birthday party." Camden's speech slurred and he swayed on his feet as he struggled to focus on his friend. "It's the only place with a reputation worse than his."

"Speaking of the devil, here come our friends now." Wittingham gestured with his tumbler to the two approaching men. "Must have lost at hazard to be back so soon."

Camden squinted. He would have to take Wittingham's word that the approaching forms were their companions; he'd be damned if he could see anything. Then they came close enough that the single blurry shape resolved into Farber and Hollsworth.

"Lost your money so soon?" Wittingham asked.

"Every last shilling," Hollsworth said with a grin.

"Good God, Camden, you look like hell," Farber said loudly as he slapped Camden on the back, causing him to spill the rest of his brandy. "You'll have to clean yourself up by tomorrow morning or your father won't let you in the shipping office. He'd never let such a haggard-looking creature serve as the factotum of his precious business."

"I have plenty of time to clean up before I must report to my father," Camden said.

Hollsworth pulled out his watch. "You have four hours, to be exact." He put the watch back in its pocket and then took in the appearance of his friend. "Not nearly enough time."

"I can't be all that bad."

Farber laughed and slapped Camden on the back again. "Your clothes are stained and crumpled, your eyes are red and blurry, you're looking a bit puffy about that pretty face of yours, and God knows where your cravat's got off to. What an impression you will make on your first day."

Camden frowned. "Perhaps I should make my way home, if I am that bad off. I'll never hear the end of it if I don't show up on time looking presentable."

"Nonsense," Wittingham said. "It is your birthday and your last night of freedom. Beginning tomorrow morning, you are forever cursed to the drudgery of employment. You might as well stay out the entire night and report to your father from here. Daddy will understand."

"Indeed," Farber said. "There is still so much to be done tonight."

"What more is there to do? You've lost all your money," Hollsworth pointed out.

"Yes, but I haven't lost Camden's money yet, so the night is not over."

Wittingham laughed. "Ah yes, how lucky were are that our friend has some of the deepest pockets in London. When we have gambled almost all his purse away tonight, we can spend the rest on whores and liquor."

"Let's not wait on the liquor," Farber said as he peered into his empty tumbler. "I am in dire need of more brandy. As is the birthday boy." Farber grabbed Camden's glass from his loose grasp and turned it upside down. "See?"

"Oh, no, Farber, no more brandy—"

"Right then. First, we get more brandy," Wittingham said, as if Camden hadn't spoken. "Then it's back to the hazard tables." He led the way through the crowd, Farber and Hollsworth close behind.

Camden stumbled along for a few steps but then stopped as a wave of nausea hit him. He had been drinking with his friends since early that evening, and had probably consumed more alcohol in that day than in all the rest of his life. His head pounded and his mouth was horribly dry, as if he had tried to swallow a bundle of cotton rags.

He suddenly wanted nothing more than to be out of Belford's club. It was too crowded and too loud and too chaotic. Too full of groups of drunk and bloated men laughing and yelling as they gambled and fought and chased the club's whores around the floor. He looked around, squinting, trying to find his friends in the blurry mass of black coats, but they had already disappeared into the crowd. It was just as well, he supposed, that he snuck out without telling them. They would never let him leave while the hazard tables were still open and there was still brandy to drink and women to grope. He would have to slip out the side door.

He changed course and pushed his way through the crowd. He pulled out his watch as he lurched along, bumping into furniture and men in his dizziness. He took the watch from its chain and brought it nearer to his eyes, but no matter how hard he squinted, he couldn't make out the time.

"Need some help, love?" a soft feminine voice asked from behind him. Camden turned to find a demimondaine sidling up to him. She was a garish creature, heavily made-up, with a thick coat of powder highlighting the lines of her face and two bright spots of rouge on her cheeks. Her lips were thin and dry, and when she spoke he could see she was missing teeth. "I can give ye the time," she said huskily. "I'll give ye all night."

Camden backed away from her. "Just tell me what that says." He took another step back and put his watch in front of her.

"Almost five," she answered, stepping close to him again.

"Dammit, Hollsworth was wrong. I have only three hours."

"Plenty o' time," the woman breathed. She backed Camden up against the wall, hitched up the skirts of her frayed and crumpled gown, and straddled one of his legs. She rubbed her breasts into his chest, running one of her hands along his torso, stopping coyly near the waistband of his trousers. His watch clattered to the floor.

"I—I must go." Camden pushed past her, not stopping until he reached the side door, and then he burst out onto the street. He stood still for a moment, trying to regain his balance and remember which way to his new townhouse. The residence was a birthday gift from his father, and he had barely moved in. He began walking down the empty street, realized he was going the wrong way, and turned around.

He had only three hours to get home, catch a little sleep, clean up, and report to his father's shipping office at eight. Contrary to what Wittingham thought, his father would most definitely *not* understand if he showed up looking anything less than impeccable and eager to work. Not the father who had once punished him for showing up at dinner with his cravat slightly off center. Not the father who drilled him daily on the importance of appearance and the necessity of increasing the Camdens' social standing to match their great wealth.

Camden quickened his gait, his boots making a sharp clipping noise against the cobblestones, and the sound echoed eerily through the empty streets. It seemed there wasn't another soul out tonight, nothing around him except the faded yellow glow of the gas streetlamps and the cold tendrils of an early morning fog. He heard a loud commotion behind him, a strange thumping punctuated by an otherworldly shriek. He whipped around to see two cats clawing and hissing at each other. He was about to turn back around and continue on his way when another struggle caught his eye. Further down the street, pressed into the shadows, a man clutched at the skirts of a woman. She slapped at him, crying, "You mustn't!" as she backed away. The man grabbed her by the upper arm and pulled her toward him, and Camden could just make out his low growl telling her he could and he would.

Camden was drunk, his vision was blurry, and he had the sensation he was moving through water. He was slow to react to what he saw, and by the time he began to walk toward them, the woman had already broken free. One of her slaps had connected soundly with the man's face and he had released her as he stumbled to the ground. She came running down the street toward Camden, passed him without noticing him, and turned down a dead-end alley. Camden glanced at the man, expecting to see him pursuing her, but he hadn't yet regained his feet. Camden decided he would first find the woman and offer her his assistance before dealing with the man.

He turned into the alley, searching the shadows until he caught movement off in the corner. She was there, standing in a dim halo of gaslight, leaning against the brick wall of a sooty building, one hand against her chest as she struggled to catch her breath.

"Madam," Camden said as he hurried to her.

The woman went still. "You aren't Lord Ashe," she said.

Camden startled at the name. He hadn't realized the man she was struggling with was Lord Ashe. He knew the man—knew *of* him, at least. Ashe was an aggressive and pompous earl who had business dealings with Camden's father. He was a man of dark temper and dark secrets, and Camden wondered how such a beautiful woman had become tangled up with him. "No, I'm Camden—Rhys Camden."

"What is it you want, Mr. Camden? Why have you followed me here?"

Camden stood a few feet from her. He stepped forward and reached for her, but stopped when he saw her draw away. "I'm not going to harm you," Camden said, and though he was trying to be reassuring, his voice sounded thick and strange to his ears. "I've come to rescue you, actually."

He expected a dramatic reaction from the woman; perhaps she would cry in relief or throw herself into his arms in gratitude. He never expected her to laugh. Her slender shoulders shook slightly, causing the fine silk of her gown to tremble, and the loose tendrils of her golden hair to bounce and sway. Camden did reach for her then, his fingertips lightly touching the smooth, cool skin of her arm.

"I'm not in need of rescue," she said.

"But I saw you struggle with Ashe. I saw you slap him and run away. Do not be frightened, madam. I will protect you from him."

A slight smile touched the woman's lips. Camden knew he should be concentrating on assisting her, but he couldn't help but notice how lovely she was. Even in the dim, hazy light of the streetlamp, he could see how the golden curls of her thick hair framed the fine, high cheekbones of her face. His gaze traveled over her plump lips the color of claret, then along the delicate bones of her neck and shoulder, and down to her full breasts. Every part of her telegraphed an ethereal, sensual beauty.

"I assure you," the woman said, bringing Camden's attention back to the present situation, "that I am not in need of any protection."

"But surely—I mean, you cannot—" Camden broke off, confused.

"It is merely a game between Lord Ashe and me, one we often play."

"A game? I do not understand."

"Lord Ashe chases me through the streets, and I struggle and run until I let him catch me."

"What is the point of such a game? To be running through the streets at this hour—"

"The point is pleasure, Mr. Camden." She leaned in closer to him, as if she were going to tell him a secret. "Have you never done anything for pleasure?"

"What can possibly be the pleasure in that?" She was so close to him now that he could feel the heat of her, smell the light scent of lavender on her hair.

The woman laughed again, and she brought a hand up to his arm, her long fingers resting lightly on his coat. There were layers of clothes between his skin and hers, yet a shiver went through him at her touch. "You are so young, Mr. Camden, so innocent," she whispered.

"I'm twenty-one," Camden said, indignant, and he drew himself up to his full height, towering over her by at least a foot. "And I'm not so very innocent."

"Yet your cheeks go red at my touch," she said, and when he started to protest, she stepped closer, until the tips of her silk-covered breasts were touching the wool of his coat. Camden hardened and his face grew hotter. He tried to step back. His erection would be apparent to her if he didn't put some distance between them, but she tightened her grasp on his arm and he found he couldn't move.

She was mesmerizing, this delicate beauty who talked of pleasure and radiated a dangerous sexuality. He was seized with the desire to kiss her, to take her plump lips in his and see if they tasted like wine. He started to lean down to her, and she watched him expectantly, lips slightly parted, until something behind him caught her attention.

"I must go," she said, dropping his arm and stepping past him. "I thank you for your concern, but I am in no need of your help."

"Wait," Camden said, not sure what to say, but knowing he didn't want her to leave.

The woman hesitated for a moment, then turned back to him, stood on her tiptoes, and pressed her lips to his cheek. He reached for her, but she was already moving away from him, her skirts swishing through the fog.

He watched her walk down the alley to the connecting street and then disappear around the corner. He followed her, nearly running down the alley to the corner. He paused, looking up and down the street until he spotted Lord Ashe chasing the woman. Even though she had told him it was just a game, he wanted to go to her and save her from her pursuer. He started to move toward her but then sank back into shadows when Lord Ashe caught her about the waist and turned her around. They were far enough away that he couldn't make out the expressions on their faces, but he could see now from the way they moved with each other that she truly didn't need his protection. She shrieked and slapped at Lord Ashe when he grabbed her, but she leaned in closer to him as she did so. Lord Ashe took her by the arms, holding her firmly, but Camden could see that there was no real roughness in his touch.

Camden knew he should leave them. They were standing down the street in the opposite direction he needed to go, and he could slip away without drawing their notice. But he found himself rooted to the spot, intrigued by this strange game played in the empty streets before dawn by a beautiful woman and a powerful man.

Lord Ashe backed the woman against a building, and said something to her in a low, husky tone. Camden saw one of Lord Ashe's large hands run up the bodice of the woman's gown, saw him run a finger along the neckline and over the curve of her breast. Camden drew in his breath, shocked that the couple would engage in such behaviors in the middle of the street, even if there were no one about. Then Camden saw Lord Ashe's bring his mouth to the woman's neck, kissing her almost aggressively.

Camden felt a strange mixture of horror and curiosity as he watched Lord Ashe thrust his hips toward the woman, lifting her off the ground. He was not completely lacking in experience with women, but none of his admittedly few encounters had prepared him for the sight of a man and woman engaging in illicit behavior on the street, in plain view of anyone who happened to come along. As an overly reserved and proper young man, he'd never thought to conduct himself in such manner; before tonight, it hadn't occurred to him that *anyone* would think to do it.

He stiffened again, shamefully aroused at the sight of the woman, at the sound of her sighs and moans as she clutched at her lover. Camden ached to touch the woman as Lord Ashe touched her, to sink himself into her, to taste her, to hear her cries against his ear—even as he was horrified at the very thought of fondling a woman in the street. The couple's movements became more frenzied, until Camden wondered if he would take her right there, but then Lord Ashe backed away from the woman, setting her gently on the ground. He removed his coat and put it around her, then leaned down to her, and Camden thought Lord Ashe said, "Let's finish this at your townhouse," as he put an arm around her waist and propelled her down the street.

Camden stood in the shadows of the street, his erection throbbing, his head pounding. He shouldn't have watched them, shouldn't have been aroused at the sight of their passion, shouldn't stand here thinking about her until he burned with unmet need. But the image of Lord Ashe and the nameless woman was still seared in his mind, and it wouldn't let him go. The couple had disappeared, yet still he stood, staring down the empty street until he became convinced it had all been just a drunken dream.